The Firefighter's Slow Burn

The Firefighter's Slow Burn

A Glacier Creek Romance

Karen Foley

The Firefighter's Slow Burn

Tule Publishing First Printing, March 2018

The Tule Publishing Group, LLC

First Publication by Tule Publishing Group 2018

ISBN: 978-1-948342-83-4

Chapter One

A LOUD COMMOTION outside the offices of *Adrenaline Adventures* made Dylan McCafferty look up from where he studied a topographical map of the mountains surrounding the small town of Glacier Creek, Montana. On the street below, a lime-green Jeep towing a shiny silver Airstream trailer tried to turn into a small side street, but the driver had misjudged the amount of clearance. In a classic rookie move, the driver had attempted to reverse out of the side street but had overcompensated. Now the Jeep and the trailer were jack-knifed at an impossible angle, completely blocking the road. Dylan might not have intervened, except the back end of the trailer was dangerously close to his Range Rover, parked along the curb.

He shot to his feet, drawing the attention of his friend and partner, Jamie Colter, who was talking on the phone with a client. Now he followed the direction of Dylan's gaze, and cupped his hand over the phone.

"Need any help?" he asked.

"No," Dylan muttered darkly. "I got this."

He took the stairs to the first floor two at a time, and

burst out onto the sidewalk, where a small crowd of spectators had begun to gather. Glacier Creek was a small town by any standards, but its proximity to Flathead Lake and Glacier National Park made it a popular tourist destination in the summer, swelling the local population. A long, shady greenway divided Main Street into two one-way streets, and a colorful explosion of quaint art galleries, gift shops, restaurants, and local businesses characterized each side of the main road. The roads converged in a small parking area next to the lake, just a few blocks down, where a long, wide pier extended out over the water.

Dylan couldn't begin to fathom why this driver had decided to bring the Airstream through the congested town center. As he saw the trailer begin to reverse—directly into his Range Rover—he hurriedly pushed his way through the crowd.

"Whoa, whoa!" he shouted, and ran to the passenger side of the Jeep, thumping his hand hard on the window.

The Jeep came to an abrupt stop, and Dylan looked through the glass to see a woman behind the wheel, her expression both alarmed and frustrated.

Dylan yanked the passenger door open. "Take your foot off the gas," he commanded, "or you're going to drive this rig right through my vehicle."

She turned to look at him, and whatever else Dylan had meant to say was completely forgotten as he found himself staring into the biggest, bluest eyes he'd ever seen, ringed in lush, black lashes. For one long, endless instant their gazes locked. Her pert, pink mouth had fallen open, and all Dylan could think was how those soft lips might feel beneath his own. The way her attention was riveted on him, Dylan knew she'd felt it too—the electric thrum of attraction passing between them was too strong to ignore.

But then she dragged her gaze from his and craned her neck to look through the open passenger door, and saw the trailer was scant inches from the Range Rover. Dylan was still trying to collect his wits, which had scattered somewhere on the floor near her feet. Jesus, she was more than just pretty—she was like something conjured out of his fantasies, with glossy, black hair cut in short layers that curled up gently at the ends, and made him want to slide his fingers through them. The long fringe of her bangs framed her face so the first thing you noticed were those amazing eyes. No makeup, either, he was sure of it. Just flawless skin, thick lashes, and those decadent lips.

He was a goner.

"Oh, sugar beets!" She thrust the Jeep into drive, but there was nowhere for her to go, wedged as she was by the surrounding cars. Realizing her predicament, she thumped her hand on the steering wheel and threw him an accusing glare, as if he were somehow to blame. "Now what am I supposed to do?"

Her voice had a husky quality to it that Dylan liked. It made him think of dark, velvet nights and hot, unhurried sex. He gave her his slow, sexy smile, the one that never failed to make the ladies go a little boneless.

"What do I get if I help you out?" he asked suggestively. "I think a kiss would be fair payment."

Her eyes widened, and her lips rounded in an "*oh*" of surprise, before they clamped tightly shut and her brows drew together in a disapproving frown.

Muffled laughter came from the back of the Jeep, and Dylan peered inside to see two young boys in the back seat, falling against each other in amusement. They shared their mother's black hair and startling blue eyes. Dylan almost tripped over himself in his hurry to step away from the Jeep.

Jesus, she was married! Even if she wasn't, she had kids.

Dylan was a firm believer in rules, and rule number one was steer clear of married women. The second rule was steer clear of women with kids. There was a reason he was still single at the ripe old age of thirty—he had no desire to be tied down. Not now. Maybe not ever. He had too many adventures left on his bucket list to be shackled to a wife and kids.

"Slide over," he said now, reluctantly discarding any thoughts of seduction. "I'll get you out of here."

The woman's expression turned to one of amusement. "What? You think you can do a better job of driving than I can?"

Dylan leaned across the passenger seat, and smiled. "Sweetheart, I know I can. Move over."

He watched as her skin flushed pink and her eyes widened. Then she looked past him to where a dozen or more people stood on the sidewalk watching in amusement. Behind her, cars were stacking up along Main Street. Nobody was blowing their horn, but it was only a matter of time before their patience wore thin.

"Fine," she muttered, and lifted herself across the center console to the passenger seat. She was so close he could see the fine blue vein at her temple, throbbing now with suppressed emotion. "She's all yours."

Rounding the front of the Jeep, he climbed behind the wheel and adjusted the seat for his longer legs. He turned to look at the boys. "Having fun, guys?"

"Yes!" the older one said, bouncing on the seat. "This is awesome!"

"Are we going to crash into that car?" This from the smaller boy, who peered out the window with an anxious expression.

"Another dent in that thing might be an improvement," the woman observed. She narrowed her gaze on Dylan. "Are you sure you know what you're doing? Because if that's your vehicle, you obviously have no idea how to drive."

The ancient Range Rover *had* seen better days, but that didn't mean it wasn't still his baby. "Those marks are called experience," he said, focusing his attention on the side mirrors. "Something you obviously don't have, or you wouldn't be in this tight spot."

She gave a small huff of mock outrage, but her eyes were smiling. "When's the last time you had your vision checked? I've had this Jeep for over a year, and there's not a mark on it. *That's* the sign of an experienced driver."

"I guess it's all in how you look at it," he said, carefully turning the wheel.

"Speaking of which…" She glanced uncertainly into her side mirror at how close the trailer was to the vehicles parked along the curb. "Maybe I should get out and guide you."

"Nope, I've got this," Dylan assured her.

"Pretty sure of yourself, aren't you?"

Dylan flashed her a grin. "Yep."

She'd left him very little room in which to maneuver the Jeep and the trailer, and it took more than a few minutes to carefully inch his way clear, but soon he was driving forward with the trailer pulling straight behind him. A cheer went up from the spectators on the sidewalk, and Dylan barely suppressed an urge to give the woman a triumphant grin. Instead, he drove to a spot several blocks up, at the end of the greenway, and pulled the vehicle over before killing the engine.

"You should be all set from here," he said, turning in his seat to face her.

Up close, she was even prettier than he'd realized, and he knew a sense of bitter disappointment that she was off-limits. Didn't it just figure?

"Thanks, I appreciate the help." She glanced back down

the road to where his Range Rover was now several blocks away. "Sorry you have such a long walk back to your car."

Dylan arched an eyebrow, unable to resist teasing her, just a little. "Do I look like I'm out of shape?"

Her eyes swept over him, and for just an instant Dylan saw awareness and something else flicker in their depths. Appreciation? His entire body tightened under that swift, cerulean scrutiny.

"No," she reluctantly admitted, and another flush of color crawled up her neck. She reached for the door handle. "Well, thanks again. I can take it from here."

Dylan found himself reluctant to leave, despite the warning bells jangling in his head. "Where are you headed?"

She hesitated. "There's a campground just on the lake—"

"I know it," Dylan said. "The Glacier Creek Campground. You'll like it there. The sites are clean and good-sized, and there's a nice little beach. I understand they have activities for the kids, too."

"Yes, that's why I chose it. Well, that and the proximity to Glacier National Park." She opened the passenger door and prepared to climb out.

"Where are you traveling from?" He didn't want her to leave. He told himself there was absolutely no point in continuing any conversation with her, but he couldn't prevent his mouth from talking.

"We're doing a cross-country road trip," she said, shooting a warning glance toward the boys, who were busy pummeling each other in the back seat. "We started our trip in Newark, New Jersey, about five weeks ago, and now here we are."

Dylan gave a low whistle. "That's a lot of driving."

"It's been a lot of fun."

She gave him a bright smile, but Dylan sensed she wasn't being entirely truthful. Had she come this far on her own, with just the boys?

"You plan on driving through the park?" He referred to nearby Glacier National Park, which was the biggest draw for most of the tourists who passed through town.

"Possibly. I'm more interested in doing some hiking in the area."

"That's great. If you stop by our office, we have plenty of trail maps for the park, and we could even provide a guide for you, if you're interested."

She sharpened her gaze on him. "What is it, exactly, you do?"

Dylan extended his hand. "I'm Dylan McCafferty—part owner of *Adrenaline Adventures*. You can't miss it; it's in the old mercantile building a few blocks back."

After a brief hesitation, she placed her hand in his, and Dylan closed his fingers around hers, admiring her firm grip. "Hayden Temple, and these two are Ollie and Jackson. I'm not sure we're up for any adrenaline-inducing adventures. Just being away from the city is enough for us."

Dylan found himself mesmerized by the tilt of her eyes.

"We also rent kayaks, bikes, and hiking gear. Why don't you stop by?" He raised his hands. "No pressure, and definitely no sales pitch. But we'd be happy to give you some tips on the best hiking trails for kids."

"Maybe—thanks." When he continued to stare at her, she gave him an expectant look as if to say, *What?*

She wore no wedding band or diamond on her left hand, and he desperately wanted to ask about any significant other, but decided he was already wading in too deep just by encouraging her to stop by the store. She had kids, and he definitely didn't need the kind of complication she represented.

Quickly, before he could say something he'd regret, he climbed out of the Jeep. "Okay, then. Nice meeting you, and enjoy your stay in Glacier Creek."

He stepped back and jammed his hands into his pockets as Hayden came around to the driver's side and climbed in. She wore a pair of khaki shorts that hugged the curves of her sweet ass, and her bare legs were toned and trim. Dylan couldn't help but notice her T-shirt did nothing to disguise the pert thrust of her small breasts. She absolutely was not his type, but every cell in his body rose to attention when she gave him a last, farewell smile.

He nodded as she put the Jeep into gear, and watched as she drove away, until finally she made a right turn toward Highway 35 along the lake, and the trailer disappeared from view. Dylan blew out a breath and scrubbed his hands over his face. He was really losing it if he even remotely considered her to be fair game. He mentally checked off all the factors working against her: possibly married, definitely a mom, lived on the other side of the country.

No question about it—she was completely off-limits.

Chapter Two

HAYDEN HAD HOPED a strenuous hike through the mountains surrounding Glacier Creek would burn off some of the boys' excess energy, but an hour into the trek, they showed no signs of slowing down. Almost against her better judgment, she had picked up a trail map at *Adrenaline Adventures*. There had been a small kiosk on the sidewalk outside the entrance, with maps and brochures of the local attractions. After some indecision, she had taken the trail map from the display and shoved it into her backpack. She didn't need to go inside the building; didn't need to run into the hunky guy who had come to her rescue three days earlier. He'd probably think she was there on a pretext, hoping to run into him again.

He'd be right.

She told herself a guy like him probably had an ego as big as Montana, and she didn't need to give him another reason to feel good about himself. So she'd taken the map from the sidewalk display, even as a part of her hoped he might make an appearance.

He didn't.

She'd been both disappointed and relieved. Disappointed, because he was hands-down the sexiest man she'd ever met. Relieved, because she was only passing through the picturesque town of Glacier Creek, and there was absolutely no chance they could ever do anything more than exchange polite greetings.

With his chiseled cheekbones and long mane of dark gold hair, he'd reminded her of a modern-day Thor. His square jaw had been covered in a scruff of golden beard, and his hazel eyes had missed nothing. Just remembering the overtly masculine look he'd given her as he'd told her to slide into the passenger seat caused shivers of awareness to spread over her skin. She considered herself an independent woman, but his take-charge attitude had thrilled her, just a little.

Now she stopped on the steep trail to catch her breath, bracing her hands on her knees as she looked upward to where her two nephews had vanished around a curve. The first part of the hike had been easy, but the last mile had required more effort, although you'd never guess by how easily the boys tackled the trail. Ollie and Jackson were a handful, but she'd been looking forward to making this trip and spending time with them. They were growing up so fast!

More importantly, she'd wanted to remove them from their volatile home environment back in New Jersey. Hayden's older sister, Molly, had recently demanded a divorce from her husband of almost twelve years, and the split couldn't be any more acrimonious. Hayden had visited her sister three months earlier, and had been sickened by how bitter the custody battle had become. She knew she had to get her nephews out of there. Thankfully, that decision had been the one thing both Molly and her husband, Steve, had agreed upon.

A middle school art teacher, Hayden had ten weeks of summer vacation. She had borrowed a friend's Airstream trailer and had set out from New Jersey five weeks earlier. So far, the trip had been both amazing and exhausting. Hayden loved her young nephews, but they delighted in getting into mischief of all kinds, and she had found out the hard way they couldn't be trusted alone, even for a few moments.

Now she straightened and determinedly began climbing the trail after them, uncomfortably aware of the sweat that trickled between her breasts and caused her tank top to cling damply to her skin beneath the backpack she carried. Her thighs burned from exertion, and her breathing came in uneven fits. The day had turned hot, and her backpack grew heavier with every step. The surrounding forest was quiet, as if even the birds had decided it was too hot to take flight. She was almost ready to turn back. The descent would go much quicker, and they could be back to the campground in plenty of time for an afternoon swim.

As she rounded an enormous boulder, the boys leaped out from behind the rock with their fiercest war cries, in an attempt to scare her. Hayden pretended fright, although she had heard them before she'd seen them.

"Oh my goodness," she said, gasping. "You really did startle me!"

The boys laughed in satisfaction, and Jackson, who had just turned eleven, pointed to a sign that marked the trail.

"Look, Auntie Hayden, this says there are bears up here!"

Ollie, who was only eight and small for his age, sucked in his breath and moved closer to Hayden. "We don't have to go any further," he said anxiously. "We could go back to the campground."

Jackson made a scoffing sound of disgust. "You're such a baby."

"Be nice to your brother." Hayden stepped closer to the sign, which marked a fork in the trail. The red sign showed a picture of a large bear, with the words, *Bear Country. All wildlife is dangerous. Do not approach or feed.* On either side of the warning were two trail markers, one for the trail they were currently on, which was the Larch Trail, and another for the second trail, which read *Eagle's Bluff Trail.*

"Where does this other trail go, Auntie Hayden?" Jackson asked.

"I'm not sure," she admitted, and shrugged her backpack off and set it on the ground. "Why don't I take a look at the map, and find out?"

Kneeling down, she fished through the contents, and pulled out the map she'd picked up earlier. Jackson bent over the backpack.

"Do you have any snacks in here?"

"You can each have a water bottle and a granola bar," she said absently. "But just one."

Jackson gave a hoot of triumph and delved into the backpack. As the boys climbed to the top of the boulder to enjoy their snack, Hayden unfolded the trail map. She spread it out on the surface of the rock, uncapped a bottle of water and drank it greedily as she studied the map. The trail they were on continued upward for another quarter of a mile or so, and then descended to the valley floor, but not anywhere near the original trailhead. If they continued on the Larch Trail, they would end up miles from where she had left the Jeep.

A sudden noise on the trail behind her startled her, and she whirled around with her heart in her throat, half expecting to see a bear, but it was only a hiker, descending from the Eagle's Bluff Trail.

Hayden almost stopped breathing.

It was him. The man from Glacier Creek.

He looked rugged and bigger than life in a pair of close-fitting hiking shorts that couldn't hide his impressive thigh muscles. He wore a T-shirt and a backpack, and a dark bandana around his head. Now he stopped and took his sunglasses off, and swept his golden gaze over her. Hayden felt the same thrill she'd felt three days ago, when he'd helped her move the Airstream.

"Hayden Temple," he said with a grin. His teeth were white against the scruff of his beard. "You are the last person

I expected to see up here."

Her insides expanded with pleasure—he remembered her name! She'd never been good at hiding her feelings, but she strove for what she hoped was a casual tone.

"Oh, hey! Daryl, right?"

"Dylan," he corrected her, but the gleam in his eyes told her he wasn't fooled by her error. "Where are the boys?"

Hayden turned toward the boulder, but the boys were nowhere to be seen. How had they crept off without her noticing? Alarm flared through her.

"Oh, sugar beets," she muttered. Then, louder, "Jackson! Oliver! Come out right now! This isn't funny!"

"How long have they been gone?" Dylan asked.

"They were right here just five minutes ago," Hayden said, indicating the boulder. "I gave them a snack, and they climbed up to the top. I was just checking the trail map…I can't believe they're gone!"

"Maybe nature called."

"No," she said quickly. "They wouldn't do that. We have a strict rule about wandering away. They know better!"

Or at least they should, she amended silently. In the last few weeks, Jackson had exhibited some defiant behavior, and had even challenged her authority on two separate occasions. She'd chalked it up to the emotional stress of being away from home while his parents went through a divorce.

"They should be okay," Dylan said in a loud voice, and picked up her backpack, "as long as they can run faster than that bear I spotted back up on the trail. C'mon, let's get out of here."

He hefted her pack over one shoulder, and as she stood holding her map and bottled water, mouth agape, there was a sudden loud commotion from the nearby trees. The boys exploded out of the dense underbrush with expressions of panic on their faces.

"No, don't leave!" Jackson cried. "We're here!"

"Wait for us!" Oliver shouted, and ran to Hayden, throwing his arms around her waist. He looked especially guilty, and Hayden felt her annoyance recede, just a little.

Dylan gave Hayden a knowing wink. "Works every time."

Jackson turned on him with an affronted look. "You mean there isn't really a bear?"

"Well, I did see a bear," Dylan confirmed, "but that was yesterday, and he was at a much higher elevation. My guess is he's a good twenty miles away by now."

"Oh, man," wailed Oliver. "You really scared me!"

Reaching out, Dylan ruffled the boy's dark hair. "You don't have to be scared, but you should always be aware of your surroundings and never, ever leave the trail without letting an adult know. Got it?"

Oliver gave his brother a swift, stricken look and then hung his head. His voice was little more than a whisper. "Yes."

"You should probably apologize to your mom for scaring

her," he continued. "That wasn't a very nice trick."

"She's our aunt," Jackson corrected him, in a tone that clearly expressed his disdain for the notion. "Not our mom."

Hayden glanced at Dylan. Was it her imagination, or did he look at her with renewed interest?

"You thought I was their mother?" she asked him in mock outrage. "Please tell me I don't look that old!"

Dylan shrugged, but had the grace to look embarrassed. "I just figured you got an early start."

"My parents are getting a divorce," Jackson said matter-of-factly. "Auntie Hayden said we should spend the summer with her, until everything's settled."

"That seems like a good idea," Dylan said carefully. "Are you having a good summer?"

Jackson shrugged. "It's okay, I guess."

"We're having a wonderful time," Hayden said quickly, and gave Oliver a cheerful smile. "Aren't we?"

He nodded dutifully. "Yeah, even if we only get to play video games for thirty minutes after supper."

"I think we're all a little road-weary," she said, feeling the need to defend the boys' lackluster reactions. "We've been traveling for over a month. In fact, I think we may stay in Glacier Creek for the next week, and just relax."

Oliver's face brightened. "Really?"

Hayden bent and gave the little boy a swift hug. "Sure. Why not?"

"C'mon, let's go," Jackson said, scuffing at the dirt with

his foot to indicate his boredom.

"Where are you headed?" Dylan asked.

Remembering she still held the trail map, Hayden snapped it open and pretended to study it. "I'm not sure. We've only been at it for an hour or so, and I don't think any of us are ready to turn back yet."

Dylan came to stand beside her, peering over her arm at the map. "Here," he said gently, and taking the map in his hands, turned it around. "You have it upside down."

Hayden flushed and told herself his nearness had nothing to do with her sudden inability to focus. "I had initially planned to stay on this trail, but I didn't realize it takes us so far from the trailhead." She glanced at Dylan. "What about this other trail, the Eagle's Bluff?"

"It's a great hike, with some stunning scenery, but it's more strenuous than this trail. I wouldn't recommend it for kids." He leaned closer and indicated a squiggly line on the map. "There're two kinds of hiking paths; the first kind is more or less maintained, and is navigable for hikers. The other kind is little more than an animal track. You'd need to be an experienced hiker to navigate some of the ridges."

Hayden tried to concentrate on the map, but all she could think was how good he smelled, like deep Montana forests and spicy deodorant and clean male. She breathed deeply, furtively.

"See the way this line doesn't curve at all?" he asked.

Hayden nodded, eyeing his hands. They were big and

square, with neat nails and, thankfully, no rings. They were strong, capable hands. For just an instant, she envisioned them on her body, touching her bare skin.

"That's because it's very steep and runs straight up the mountain, with no switchbacks," Dylan explained, unaware of where her thoughts strayed. "Animals tend to take direct routes, and this trail is pretty untamed. There's been literally no maintenance."

"That's where you just came from?" Hayden asked, forcing her thoughts back to the map.

"I didn't go all the way up. The route has been closed for the last two years, but it just recently reopened." He paused. "My recommendation would be to hike to this point, here." He indicated a spot about a mile up the trail. "There's a nice waterfall and a swimming hole that used to be a popular destination for day hikers. There were a few people there when I passed it, but it's not crowded. Beyond that, the trail becomes much more difficult."

Jackson's head snapped up. "A waterfall? Can we go, Auntie Hayden, please?"

Hayden hesitated. They hadn't brought any towels with them, and she didn't want to spend too much time swimming, and risk being on the trail after dark. She looked at Dylan.

"How long would it take us to get there?"

Dylan rubbed a hand over the back of his neck as he considered. "No more than twenty minutes."

"Let's go!" Jackson pleaded. "It's so hot, it would be great to swim under a waterfall!"

"Yeah, let's go," Oliver echoed, and tugged on Hayden's shirt. He seemed especially eager to be back on the trail, and Hayden didn't miss how his gaze kept returning to the forest where he and Jackson had been hiding. Had he seen something that spooked him?

Hayden couldn't resist the entreaty in their blue eyes. "Okay," she relented. "We'll go, but we're only going to stay for an hour, okay? Then we need to head back."

"Yes!" Jackson fist-pumped the air.

"An hour," she repeated. "Not an hour and fifteen minutes, and not two hours. Just an hour. Promise me now you won't give me a hard time when I say we need to leave."

"We promise!" Oliver said, giving her a winning smile.

"Promise!" Jackson said.

As the boys made a dash for the trail marked Eagle's Bluff, Hayden folded the map and stowed it in her backpack, before shrugging it back on.

"Thanks for the tip," she said to Dylan, and grinned. "Looks like we're going swimming."

"No problem." He squinted through the trees overhead. "You know, if you don't mind, I think I'll hike back with you. I could use a swim."

Hayden couldn't keep her eyes from straying to the sign behind him. *All wildlife is dangerous*. She had a niggling sense that this man might be even more dangerous, at least to her rampant imagination.

"Really?" she asked. "But you just came from there. You could have gone for a swim then."

"Ah," he said with a charming smile, "but I didn't have your company then."

Feeling inexplicably lighter and more cheerful, Hayden fell into step beside him as they followed the boys up the new trail. She told herself Dylan was only being friendly; his sudden decision to spend the afternoon with them didn't mean anything. But as she listened to him talk easily about the surrounding area and the wildlife they might see, she found herself wishing she could stay in Glacier Creek for longer than just a week.

Chapter Three

THE WATERFALL WAS even more spectacular than Hayden had imagined, gushing over a forty-foot-high cliff into a deep pool at the bottom, before running off into a shallow, rocky river with a happy gurgle. Sunlight filtered in through the overhanging trees, and the water was clear enough to see the copper-colored pebbles that sat on the bottom of the pool, gleaming like hidden treasure. Surrounded by boulders and lush forest, it felt like a secret grotto.

But the real attraction of the day—one she wasn't likely to forget—had been Dylan as he'd pulled his shirt off. Hayden had nearly choked on the water she'd been drinking. His chest and shoulders were thick with muscle, and he'd sported an impressive eight-pack. Every inch of him was golden, as if he spent most of his time outdoors.

Naked.

A thick, black tribal tattoo began on the big, rounded muscle of his left shoulder and swirled its way over the bulge of his bicep. Hayden had never been a big fan of ink, but her fingers itched to trace the contours of Dylan's tattoo. If she were honest with herself, her fingers itched to explore every inch of his incredible body, and discover if he had any other hidden tattoos.

"Thank you so much for showing this to us," she said now, as she and Dylan lounged on a flat rock by the edge of the pool, half hidden behind some low brush. The boys splashed noisily in the water, along with a half dozen or so other hikers who had found the lure of the cold mountain water irresistible.

"My pleasure," Dylan said drowsily.

He lay flat on his back on the rock with his arms bent beneath his head, his eyes closed. Hayden tried—and failed—not to stare at him. He had stripped down to just his shorts, but the stretchy material did little to disguise his powerful thigh muscles…and other attributes. Her gaze crept higher, taking in his cobbled abdomen, and pectorals. Except for a narrow strip of white above his waistband, his skin was the color of warm toast. Even his underarm hair was golden.

Now he cracked one eyelid and peered up at her. Hayden snapped her gaze back to the water. He gave a groan and sat up, leaning forward to drape his arms over his bent knees.

"I can't remember the last time I did anything like this," he commented.

"Maybe you need a vacation," Hayden suggested, eyeing him cautiously.

"Maybe."

He angled his head to look at her and the sunlight in his

hazel eyes made them look like deep, clear pools of golden water, not unlike the mountain stream that rushed away from the grotto.

"Don't move," he said quietly.

His gaze rested on her mouth for a moment, before traveling over her face. Then he leaned toward her, ever so slightly.

Afterward, Hayden didn't know what had gotten into her, but she leaned toward him, her lips parted, eyelids drifting closed. She was unprepared when he reached out to gently lift something from her damp hair. He opened his hand to reveal a tiny butterfly resting on his palm.

"Oh!" Hayden exclaimed. "I didn't realize—I thought—" She watched as the little creature fluttered away. She was flustered by how she had completely misinterpreted his intentions. "I'm sorry."

In answer, Dylan leaned over and slid a hand along her jaw, turning her face to his. His lips brushed across hers in a kiss so brief and so light it left her staring at him, wanting more.

"That was a butterfly kiss," he murmured, and a smile tilted one corner of his mouth.

His hazel eyes were warm, and the dark stubble on his jaw glinted gold in the sunlight. Without conscious thought, Hayden raised her hand and gently rubbed her fingertips across the roughness of his cheek, mesmerized by the texture. His mouth was decadent, fashioned purely for pleasure.

Fastening her gaze on his lips, she leaned forward and kissed him. This was no butterfly kiss; she pressed her mouth softly against his and then touched the tip of her tongue against his mouth, teasing the seam of his lips.

He stilled, then made a low sound of approval before he slanted his mouth across hers, feasting on her with deep, hungry licks. Whatever Hayden had expected, it wasn't the heat and urgency he now returned. He overwhelmed her senses, consumed her, and she went boneless in surrender. Ribbons of desire unfurled low in her womb, and her breasts tightened beneath the thin fabric of her T-shirt. His big hand was in her hair, cradling her scalp and angling her face for better access, and she gave it to him.

Leaning in to him, she curled a hand around his neck. Her fingers stroked over his heated skin as she tried to catch his tongue, to draw him inside as far as possible, shivering with the sheer pleasure of it.

Abruptly, Dylan released her.

Hayden stared at him, her breathing uneven. He looked a little stunned, and his breath came in soft pants. He quickly put some space between them. Turning his gaze to the waterfall, he pushed a hand through his hair, shoving it back from his forehead. Hayden had an almost irresistible urge to touch him, and instead curled her hand at her side. Her body still hummed with need. With his size and coloring, he reminded her of a big, modern-day Viking. If that kiss was any indication, she wouldn't mind if he did a little plundering of her. Alarmed by the direction of her thoughts and feeling a little dazed by the intensity of the kiss, she cast around for a safe topic.

"What did you do to your leg?" she asked, indicating the long, vertical scar that stretched over his knee.

He shifted his attention to his leg and rubbed a thumb over the scar. "I shattered my kneecap jumping into a tree a few years year ago."

Hayden glanced uncertainly at him, but he wasn't joking. "What do you mean? How do you jump into a tree?"

"Very carefully," he said, with a rueful grin. "I used to be a smoke jumper with the forest service. I was jumping a fire in Idaho, but a rogue wind caught my chute and carried me into a copse of trees. Busted my leg up pretty good."

Hayden stared at him with a newfound respect. She'd never met a smoke jumper, but with the wildfires raging around the country, she'd seen plenty of them on the evening news.

"Wow," she said now. "I'm so sorry. Do you still, er, jump fires?"

"I'm still with the Glacier Creek base, but only on a voluntary basis. The injury put me out of commission for a few months, and then this opportunity to start an extreme adventure business with a couple of buddies came up, so I jumped at it." He gave her a wry smile. "No pun intended."

"But you're fully recovered?" she persisted.

"Definitely." He demonstrated by extending and bending his leg a few times. "No problem."

His legs were long and well muscled, and gilded with hair. Hayden wondered what they would feel like rubbing against her own, smoother legs. She pushed hastily to her feet.

"It's getting late, and we've been here for longer than an hour," she said. "I'm going to call the boys in. We should get going."

Reaching up, he caught her wrist in his big hand. "Hey," he said quietly. "If I upset you, I apologize. I hope you're not heading back because of me." His gaze was steady, intent.

"No," she denied quickly. She made a dismissive gesture with one hand, as if exchanging deep, hot kisses with a guy she barely knew was an everyday, common occurrence. "Of course not!"

"Okay, good."

He released her wrist, but Hayden could still feel the warmth of his fingers on her skin. Shading her eyes against the glare of sun on the water, she called the boys' names.

"Ollie is having fun now," she said, feeling the need to explain, "but he doesn't have a lot of stamina. He'll be exhausted going down the mountain, and I can't carry him and my backpack."

"I'll carry him."

Hayden cast him an amused look. "How? You have a backpack, too."

"Trust me," he said, "I can carry both."

His tone said he was stating fact, and not bragging, or trying to impress her. With his physique and powerful legs, she guessed he would have little trouble in carrying both Ollie and his pack. There was a part of Hayden that wanted to stay with Dylan, to spend time with him, and enjoy both his attention and his touch. But another part of her was afraid she wanted more, which was impossible. She had her nephews to think about, and she would be leaving Glacier Creek in just a few, short days.

Reluctantly, it seemed, Dylan gathered up his belongings and pushed to his feet. Hayden watched furtively as he pulled his shirt on. The guy was so insanely hot that it hurt to look at him. She'd been surprised by his willingness to spend the afternoon with her and the boys, but he'd seemed to genuinely enjoy himself. He'd spent most of the time in the water with Ollie and Jackson, showing them tricks and tossing them around. And once, when Hayden had swum too close, he'd picked her up and tossed her in, too. She could still feel his big hands around her waist, lifting her as if she weighed no more than Ollie.

The boys swam over to their rock, and Hayden knew immediately they weren't happy about leaving.

"Auntie Hayden," Jackson implored, "can't we stay for just a little bit longer?"

"We had a deal," she said firmly. "One hour, and you wouldn't complain. I've let you stay for much longer than an hour, and now it's time to head back."

Jackson slapped at the water to communicate his displeasure, but Hayden ignored him. Leaning down, she helped lift Ollie onto the rock, and rubbed him down briskly with a spare sweatshirt she'd brought.

"C'mon out, bud," Dylan said, and extended a hand to Jackson. "Your aunt doesn't want to be out here after dark, so we need to make sure she gets back safely. It's what men do, right?"

Jackson sighed, but took Dylan's hand and allowed himself to be lifted out of the water and onto the rock. "I guess," he muttered, "but trust me when I say Auntie Hayden isn't afraid of anything, especially not the dark. If anything, you should be afraid of *her*."

"Thanks, Jackson," Hayden said approvingly, and gave the boy a fist-bump. She couldn't help but swagger a little as she looked at Dylan. "Tell me again what it is men do?"

Dylan chuckled and bent to retrieve his hiking boots and socks. "Sweetheart," he murmured into her ear, "I'd much rather show you."

Hayden's gaze flew to his even as heat bloomed low in her center at the suggestion in his voice, but he just grinned and sat down on a nearby boulder to pull on his socks and boots. Hayden found she couldn't quite catch her breath. She began gathering the boys' clothing, but couldn't resist watching Dylan furtively. Jeez, even his feet were gorgeous...and big. Her sister had once told her you could tell a lot about a man by the size of his feet. If that were true...

"Where are my shorts?" Jackson asked.

The boys had gone swimming in just their Marvel-themed underwear, and now Hayden reached over to pick up their shorts from where she had left them on the rock. As she shook Jackson's shorts out, something fell out of his pocket and landed on the rock.

Reaching down, Hayden retrieved three wooden matchsticks.

"Jackson, where did you get these?"

Jackson snatched his shorts from her hand and began shoving his legs into them, not looking at her. "I don't know," he finally said. "I guess I found them."

Hayden frowned. "Where did you find them?"

"I don't remember," he said, avoiding her eyes. "Why are you making such a big deal out of it?"

"Because it is a big deal," Hayden said firmly. She waited until he'd buttoned his shorts, and then took him by both arms, dipping her head to look directly into his eyes. "If I thought you were playing with matches, I would be very, very concerned."

"Well, I'm not," he finally muttered.

Hayden released him, and looked over at Ollie, who had pulled his shorts on, and was studiously tugging his socks on. She'd found when she couldn't get information out of Jackson, she could usually appeal to Ollie to come clean.

"Ollie, do you know anything about this?"

Ollie didn't look at her, just shook his head.

Hayden closed her hand around the loose matchsticks and put them in her own pocket. "Okay, I'm going to trust neither of you have been irresponsible."

She glanced at Dylan, who was watching the boys carefully. She'd thought, since he was a firefighter, that he might add his own thoughts about the danger of playing with matches, but he kept silent.

"We have to hike back in wet underwear?" Jackson asked, a note of petulance in his tone.

"Well, you refused to come out of the water in time to let them dry, so I guess so," Hayden replied. At his dejected expression, she ruffled his hair. "Don't worry, they'll dry quickly in this heat."

Hayden had gone for a quick swim in her shorts and T-shirt when they'd first arrived at the waterfall, but then she'd opted to lounge on the nearby rocks, specifically so her clothes would dry in time for the hike back to town. She was mostly dry, but the waistband and crotch of her shorts were still damp, and she was sure she'd have a rash by the time they reached the campground.

Once the boys were dressed, she pulled on her own socks and boots, and then repacked the remnants of the lunch she'd brought with them. As she replaced the lunch bags, she checked to see if her emergency first aid tin was still at the bottom of the backpack, but couldn't find it. The small tin contained Band-Aids, antiseptic ointment, aspirin, and assorted other first aid items. It also contained a small box of wooden matches exactly like the kind that had fallen out of Jackson's pocket.

She dug deeper, but the tin box was gone. She glanced over at the boys, but they were sitting with their backs to her, talking in whispers. Had Jackson taken the tin when she'd allowed him to retrieve the snacks, back at the boulder? If he had, why would he lie about it? A deep sense of unease settled over her heart.

"Okay," she said, zipping the pack closed and swinging it over her shoulders. "I'm ready."

"Is everything okay?" Dylan asked quietly, as he came to stand beside her. "You're upset."

"They're lying to me," she said beneath her breath. "I think they took a first aid tin out of my backpack, and that's where Jackson got the matches."

"He seems like a sensible kid," Dylan assured her, keeping his voice low. "I'm sure he didn't do anything stupid."

Hayden gave him a tolerant look. "He's a prepubescent boy. Stupid comes naturally."

"Let's give him the benefit of the doubt."

Hayden nodded, then drew in a deep breath and expelled it slowly. "I'll have a talk with him when we get back to the campground. How long do you think it will take to get to the trailhead?"

Dylan checked his sports watch. "We'll take it easy, so no more than an hour is my guess."

"Well, I really appreciate you showing us the waterfall,

and that you're willing to hike back down with us," she said. "I wasn't expecting that."

"Trust me, it was my pleasure," he said. "C'mon boys, on your feet."

They groaned their protest, still unhappy at having to leave the waterfall, but obediently got to their feet and began walking up the steep embankment toward the trail. Hayden watched Dylan stride easily up the sharp incline, admiring the impressive bulge of calf muscle in his toned legs. The guy was supremely fit, and Hayden had the sense he didn't spend a lot of time in a gym—his physique was honed through sheer physical activity. He reached the top of the ridge and turned to look back at her.

"C'mon, sweetheart," he said, and extended a hand to her. "After this, it's all downhill."

Reaching up, Hayden took his hand and let him pull her the last few steps up the slope, until she stood beside him on the trail. She told herself her breathlessness had more to do with the stress of the climb, than it did his touch. The boys had already started down, and now Hayden fell into step beside Dylan, who adjusted his longer stride to match hers.

"Did you mean what you said when you told the boys you were going to stay in Glacier Creek for a while?" he asked cautiously.

Hayden glanced at him, but his eyes were hidden behind his sunglasses and she couldn't read his expression.

"Yeah," she said. "I think so. We've rarely spent more

than two or three nights in any one place, and I think it's starting to wear on all of us. Glacier Creek seems like a really sweet town, and I wouldn't mind spending a little more time here."

"What is it you do, that you can spend an entire summer on the road?" he asked. "Are you a teacher?"

"I am," she confirmed.

"Let me guess." He gave her a thoughtful look. "Music?"

Hayden laughed. "Sadly, no. I don't have a musical bone in my body. I teach art and drama at the middle school level. I usually take a bartending job at the beach during the summer, just to make a little extra money, but I thought it would be nice to spend some time with the boys."

"Do you live in Newark?"

"No!" Hayden pulled a face. "I don't like the city. I live in Maryland, just across the bay from Annapolis."

She didn't much like where she currently lived, either, but she didn't say so to Dylan. She had grown up in the country and that was where she felt most comfortable. But she hadn't lived in a rural setting since she was a teenager. Despite having lived in Maryland for the past six years, she hesitated to call it *home*. There hadn't been any place that felt like home to Hayden, not since she was fourteen years old. Sometimes she wondered if such a place even existed. Maybe it did for some: people with families and kids and white picket fences.

Just not for her.

"So the boys' parents are splitting up?"

Hayden nodded. "Yes. My sister, Molly, is older than I am, and she and Steve have been married for about twelve years. They met when Molly was in high school; she had barely graduated when they tied the knot. I was surprised when she told me she'd asked Steve for a divorce. I'd no idea their marriage was in trouble."

"That's rough," Dylan said sympathetically.

"Yeah. I think Steve never saw it coming, and now he's determined to hurt Molly as much as she's hurt him." She gave him a wry smile. "Honestly, he's kind of a dick, and I think my sister is better off without him. But now he says he wants full custody of the boys, and is trying to portray her as an unfit mom."

"Is she?"

Hayden paused. "I don't think so. We're not that close, so I don't see her very often. She's a waitress at a nice restaurant, and has been there for years. She makes good money. She works long hours, but she's a great mom."

"What about him?"

"I guess he does okay. He has a job at one of the big cargo ports in Newark, and he's really into his motorcycle, but the boys love him." She shrugged. "I can't figure it out, and Molly doesn't share much with me."

"Did one of them cheat?"

"I don't know."

She and Molly had never been all that close due to the

difference in their ages. Then, when Hayden had been fourteen years old, their father had died. Hayden didn't like thinking of that terrible time, or the impact his death had had on their family, and on her relationship with her sister.

Molly had been seventeen years old, and had been dating Steve, who had been twenty-one. Their parents had strongly disapproved of the relationship, partly because Steve was so much older, and partly because of his reckless attitude. They had been sure he would bring nothing but trouble to their lives, and they'd been partly right. After their father's death, Molly had revealed she was pregnant. She'd married Steve and they'd moved to New Jersey, where Steve had found a job moving shipping containers onto the big cargo ships. Soon after, Jackson had been born. Becoming a mother had not brought Molly closer to Hayden; it had made her more determined to keep her at arm's length.

Hayden understood.

Dylan seemed on the verge of saying something when there was a sudden commotion on the trail ahead of them. Two middle-aged women ran toward them, waving their arms. Ollie and Jackson stepped aside to let them pass, wearing identical expressions of astonishment.

"Go back, go back!" the first woman shouted, sounding panicky. "Don't go down there!"

"Why?" Dylan demanded. "What is it?"

"*Wildfire!*"

Chapter Four

"THE FLAMES ARE spreading up the mountain, and moving fast!" the second woman added. "Don't go down there. We're going to head up this way, away from the fire."

"How far down the trail is it?" Dylan asked.

"I don't know, maybe half a mile!"

Before Dylan or Hayden could question the women further, they continued running up the trail, toward the waterfall. Dylan quickly shrugged his large pack off and set it on the ground.

"Boys, come here," he commanded, and his voice brooked no argument. "I want the three of you to return to the swimming hole and wait for me. Leave my pack here. I'll be back in fifteen minutes."

"Where are you going?" Hayden couldn't keep the anxiety out of her voice.

"I have to see for myself what's happening. If the fire is as bad as those women say, I'll need to contact the forest service. Go back to the falls and wait for me there."

Without waiting to see if they obeyed, he turned and

began running down the trail. A sense of dread settled over Hayden. Had the boys caused this? What if the fire really was as bad as the women stated? What if they couldn't get back to town? What if they were trapped by the advancing flames?

As if in answer to her fears, she caught a whiff of smoke and further down the trail, she could actually see the first fingers of smoky air begin to curl through the trees.

"Oh my God," she breathed, and grabbed Dylan's pack, hefting it over one shoulder as she quickly herded the boys ahead of her.

"What is it, Auntie Hayden?" Ollie asked, his voice tremulous with fear. "Is it a fire? Did someone start a fire?"

"I don't know," Hayden replied, glancing over her shoulder at where the smoke was growing thicker. She put her hand on Ollie's shoulder and herded him ahead of her. "Just keep going, okay? We'll be safe at the waterfall."

"What about Dylan?" This from Jackson, who paused to look back to the spot where Dylan had vanished.

"He'll be fine," Hayden assured him. "He's a firefighter and his specialty is fighting wildfires, so he'll know what to do to stay safe. C'mon, keep going."

They reached the waterfall, and the women who had first alerted them were talking urgently to an older man and his adult son, while a group of teenagers clambered out of the water and began toweling off, their expressions uncertain.

"Maybe we should try to head down the mountain ourselves," one teen said to her friend. "We could just follow the stream, right?"

"Oh, no, please don't do that," Hayden said quickly, dropping Dylan's backpack onto a nearby rock. "Wildfires can be unpredictable, and there's no guarantee the stream would keep you safe. My friend just went down the trail to get a better look. He's with the forest service, and he knows all about wildfires, so we'll be safe with him."

Hayden realized she did feel safe with Dylan. She barely knew him, but she would stake her life on the fact he would keep her and the boys safe. He would keep them all safe.

Ollie stayed close to her side, but Jackson stood a little apart, keeping an eye out for Dylan. Guilt and anxiety were written all over his thin face. Watching him pace, it was all Hayden could do to hold back her tears. If the boys were responsible, there would be hell to pay.

Thirteen of them waited for Dylan to return: six teenagers who looked to be about fifteen or sixteen years old, the two older women who had alerted them to the fire, and the two men. Then there was Hayden and the boys. Taking Jackson's arm, she pulled them both aside, where the others wouldn't overhear.

"Jackson," she said urgently, "I need to know the truth. Did you and Ollie start that fire?"

"I don't know!" Jackson said, his expression anxious.

"What do you mean? Were you lighting matches?" She gave the boy a light shake. "Answer me!"

"He was lighting them and throwing them away!" Ollie said, his voice high and panicked. "Are we in trouble, Auntie Hayden? Are they going to arrest us?"

"Oh my God," Hayden breathed, staring at Jackson in horror. "Please tell me you did not do that."

He looked at her, and suddenly he was just a small, terrified boy. "I did," he whispered. "But I never saw any fire. They just went out when they hit the ground, I swear!"

He burst into tears.

Fear, swift and hot, swamped Hayden; nearly drove her to her knees. She wasn't afraid of the wildfire—she was afraid of what might happen to Jackson and Oliver when the truth came out. She knew firsthand how people would react if they discovered the boys had started the wildfire by playing with matches. As a young teenager, she'd been in their shoes. She knew the court of public opinion was merciless. Now she hugged Jackson and murmured words of assurance until he finally calmed down. Pulling out of her embrace, he swiped at his eyes. The trust in his expression when he looked at her almost undid her.

"Okay," she said, forcing herself to remain calm. "Tell me everything. What you did with the metal tin? Did you leave it in the woods?"

Jackson shook his head. "I don't know. Am I in trouble?"

Hayden struggled to think. She felt certain the boys had started the wildfire, and she knew a fire investigation team would come to the same conclusion, especially when they discovered the tin. She'd already told Dylan the boys were lying to her about taking the tin, so the entire story was bound to come out eventually. She just wished she knew a way to keep the boys' names out of it. They were so young.

"We'll worry about that later," she said, and gave them each a reassuring hug. "The important thing now is to stay safe, right? We'll tell the police what happened when we get back to town. It will be okay."

"Dylan knows," Jackson said uncertainly. "Will he be mad at me?"

"Of course not," Hayden said. "He'll know you didn't mean to start a fire. You just made a bad decision, right?"

Jackson nodded, his expression anxious.

"Here he comes!" Ollie said in excitement, pulling at her arm.

Hayden turned to see Dylan jogging toward them, and his expression said it was bad. Hayden felt her chest tighten with dread. He reached their side, a little winded. The others in the group moved closer.

"We need to move," he said in a low voice, his tone grim. "The fire has completely blocked the trail, and it's spreading fast. We're not going to be able to stay here."

"But the waterfall…the pool…won't we be safe here?" Hayden asked.

Dylan peered upward at the lush green embankment, and the trees growing on the perimeter of the surrounding cliffs. "I don't think so," he said. "When those trees go up in flames—and they will—this whole area is going to be engulfed in smoke and fire. We're better off keeping ahead of it."

"But where does this trail go?" Hayden asked.

"It brings you to the summit, but about four miles further up, we can cut across to another trail that will bring us back down to the valley floor, about twelve miles away."

"That's sixteen miles!" Hayden gasped. "The boys will never be able to hike that far! I'm not sure I can make it that far!"

"I'll be there to help you. We need to stay ahead of the fire, and maybe they can send a helicopter in to get us out before nightfall." He tipped his head down and looked directly into her eyes, and what Hayden saw in those hazel depths told her this was deadly serious. "But we need to move now."

Hayden nodded. "Okay. Of course."

Dylan quickly assembled the teens and adults around him and explained what he had seen.

"This fire is growing by the second, and it's going to be on top of us before we know it," he said. "Our only choice is to keep moving. If we can reach the Thunder Wolf Trail before dark, there's a chance the forest service can send someone up to get us, or air-drop whatever supplies we need to get us through the night."

"We're going to spend the night on the mountain?" asked one girl, her voice incredulous. "My mother is going to kill me! I didn't even tell her where I was going when I left the house this morning!"

The adult son, who Hayden had guessed was about thirty years old, stepped forward. His expression was belligerent. "Why should we trust you? The trail we came up is an easy hike. We should be able to skirt the fire and get back down!"

Dylan raised his hands. "Please, I understand your concerns, but we don't have time to argue about this, at least not here. I've been with the forest service for over ten years, the last five years as a smoke jumper with the Glacier Creek base. I've seen my share of wildfires, and this one is still in its infancy. But we've experienced a hot summer and the forest floor is very dry. It's not going to take long for this thing to turn into a monster. A fire will burn faster uphill, and when it hits a ten-degree slope it will double in speed. We're talking a wildfire that can travel at ten kilometers per hour, and unfortunately we're directly in its path." He looked directly at the other man. "So we need to get going. Agreed?"

The man stared at Dylan for a long moment, but then he nodded and began gathering his belongings, talking in a low voice to his father. One of the teenagers approached Dylan.

"Hey, we just came up here for the day." He indicated his five companions. "We've tried to call our parents, but there's no cell reception and they're going to worry."

Dylan clapped the youth on his shoulder. "I have a radio in my pack and I'm going to call the forest service now. Once we're in a safe place, you can give them your names and phone numbers, and they'll contact your families, okay?"

"Yeah, okay. Thanks."

"All right, everyone," Dylan said, raising his voice to be heard, "we're going to head up this trail, and we're going to move fast." He pointed to the older man. "You're going to go first and I'll take up the rear. Let's go."

Hayden and the boys walked quickly near the front of the line. Dylan took up the rear position, and Hayden could hear him speaking into his handheld unit, giving the approximate size and location of the wildfire. A sense of urgency permeated the entire group. As they left the waterfall, Hayden looked back and she could actually see the orange glow of flames through the distant trees, and hear the crackle of the fire as it consumed the underbrush and forest in its path. Smoke had already begun to settle over the pool and she realized Dylan had been right—remaining at the waterfall wasn't an option.

As they climbed steadily higher, the smell and sounds of the wildfire faded until finally Dylan called for everyone to stop and take a quick rest.

Hayden sat on a fallen tree with the boys and shared a bottle of water as she watched Dylan radio their new position to the fire crews. The teenagers stood in a tight cluster nearby, their damp towels draped over their shoulders, as Dylan repeated their names and phone numbers into the walkie-talkie.

Finally, he switched the radio off and turned to face the

group. "The forest service agrees we should hike up to Eagle Rock, and then make our way overland to the Thunder Wolf Trail. We have a lot of territory to cover before nightfall. How is everyone doing?"

Everyone nodded or gave him a thumbs-up, indicating they were ready to push on. The surrounding forest was still too dense for Hayden to get a sense of how high they might be, or how much distance they'd put between themselves and the wildfire. But Dylan hadn't exaggerated when he'd said the trail beyond the waterfall was difficult. They'd only been hiking for about forty minutes, but already her calves and thighs felt tight and crampy. She longed to pull out her trail map and ask Dylan to show her where they were, but he seemed anxious to get moving. So she stowed the remainder of the water, and they began hiking again.

Chapter Five

DYLAN SENT UP a silent thanks that he'd opted to spend the afternoon with Hayden Temple and her nephews, even as he regretted running into them too late to prevent the boys' mischief with the matches. But if he had continued down the trail to Glacier Creek, and allowed her to continue hiking without him, there was no saying what might have become of her and the boys, never mind the rest of their small group.

When he'd jogged back down the trail to check out the wildfire, he'd heard a low rumbling and recognized the sound of wildfire. Still, he'd been stunned by what he'd seen. He'd rounded a curve in the trial and encountered a wall of heat and flames racing along the forest floor and wicking up the tree trunks to the overhead canopy. Chunks of flaming debris fell all around, and the smoke had been thick and choking. As a wildland firefighter, he'd known what to do in order to knock back the flames, but he didn't have any of the necessary equipment. He didn't have his Pulaski,-a handheld tool that resembled an ax, and could be used to help create a firebreak or clear a trail-or a team of twenty men who could cut a fire line and clear the surrounding area of duff and other potential fuel. All he had was a radio.

Knowing how unreliable the cell phone reception was in the mountains, he always carried a two-way radio with him when he hiked, but he'd left it in his backpack, which he'd dumped on the side of the trail half a mile back. He'd sprinted back to the spot where he'd left Hayden, only to find she had brought his pack with her when she'd retreated to the waterfall.

Getting Hayden and the other hikers to safety had been his first priority. By his estimate, the wildfire had been underway for at least three hours, almost from the moment he'd encountered Hayden on the trail. Under the current conditions, given the hot, dry summer they'd been having, it wouldn't take long for the blaze to explode out of control. He was afraid it already had.

He suspected Jackson had started the wildfire while playing with matches, and he didn't know how to feel about that. The smoke jumper in him wanted to see the boy punished to the full extent of the law for his foolish and irresponsible actions. Another part of him wanted to blame Hayden for not watching the boys closely enough. But then he recalled the stricken look on both Jackson and Hayden's faces, and he had a tough time placing any blame at all. They both were obviously devastated and frightened.

Regardless, he would need to report what he knew to the authorities. Not for the first time, he wished Clay Willard wasn't the police chief in Glacier Creek. Chief Willard was, in his estimation, a bully who enjoyed the misfortune of others. Rumor had it he'd been involved in some shady dealings of his own, although nothing had ever been proven. Despite the complaints levied against him, Chief Willard had retained his position, and he wielded his authority with a heavy hand.

Dylan would do what he could to ensure Hayden and her nephews wouldn't have to deal with Chief Willard. The U.S. Forest Service would handle the investigation and possibly any subsequent charges. Jackson was just a boy, probably only eleven or twelve. The courts would likely go easy on him. But what if they didn't? What if he was sent to juvie? An experience like that, on top of his parents' divorce, could ruin his life.

Then there was Hayden, whom he found far too attractive. He'd recognized the look on her face when he'd captured the butterfly. She had thought he intended to kiss her, and so he had. He told himself he'd only done so in order not to leave her hanging, but he knew the truth.

He'd *wanted* to kiss her.

He'd been dying to kiss her since he'd first encountered her on the trail. When she'd leaned forward to kiss him, he'd been incapable of stopping her. As kisses went, it hadn't been nearly enough to slake his hunger for her, and only the presence of the boys and the other hikers had prevented him from laying her back on the warm rock and exploring that pink mouth more completely.

He liked Hayden Temple.

A lot.

Under different circumstances, he'd already be figuring a way to get her into his bed.

And that complicated things, especially since there was a high likelihood she could be held liable for not supervising the boys more closely. If he was smart, he'd distance himself from her now. Unfortunately, he'd never been very smart, especially where pretty women were concerned.

They reached the landmark called Eagle Rock in just under three hours. The going had been slow and difficult as the hiking trail had deteriorated into little more than a deer path, and the incline grew steeper. They'd had to take frequent breaks as the older folks grew winded, or just ran out of steam. Dylan worried at the rate they were going, the wildfire would overtake them.

The enormous boulder called Eagle Rock nearly blocked the haphazard trail, with a rocky outcropping that resembled the head and hooked beak of an eagle. Dylan knew the small group was tired. The older man, whose name he'd learned was Richard Madden, looked exhausted. His son, Wesley, had barely left Hayden's side during the trek, much to Dylan's annoyance. He didn't know the man, but he knew his type. Smooth and suave, and overly confident of his own appeal.

For four long miles he'd watched as the man hiked

alongside Hayden, talking to her and then insisting on carrying her backpack, even as his elderly father struggled to carry his own. He'd been overly friendly to the boys, as if he instinctively knew he had to win their approval if he was to have any chance with Hayden. His smarmy manner set Dylan's teeth on edge.

Now he watched as Wesley eased himself down on the side of the trail beside Hayden, and the rest of the group collapsed onto the ground with groans of exhaustion. Dylan stepped away and made another call to the Glacier Creek base, keeping an eye on the boys in case they should decide to wander.

"Jacqui, it's Dylan," he said, as the dispatcher answered the call.

"Where are you, Dylan? Sam says the fire has spread, and it's moving fast. They have helicopters spotting the fire, and they've sent in three different ground crews. But, Dylan—" She paused.

"What is it?"

"The aircrews spotted a second fire over by Birch Gulch. We might not have known about it for days except we were monitoring the Flat River fire."

"Is that what they're calling the fire that's chasing us?" Dylan asked. "The Flat River fire?"

"Dylan." Jacqui's voice was urgent. "Those two fires are closing in on either side of you. The size of the second blaze has more than doubled in less than two hours. If you're at

Eagle Rock, the first wildfire is less than a mile behind you and spreading fast. If you can't make it to the Thunder Wolf Trail by nightfall, you could be in trouble. You don't want to be caught in the middle when those two fronts converge. If you can't move them across to Thunder Wolf, your only other option is to go to the summit."

Dylan was silent for a moment, digesting what she'd said. This was worse—much worse—than he could have imagined.

"Jacqui," he said carefully, lowering his voice. "I have three senior citizens and two children in my group. The trail to the summit is straight up. They'll never make it."

"Then you'd better get them over to Thunder Wolf," she replied. "Sam says he'll do what he can to air-drop supplies to you tonight, and he's sending a team to meet you on the trail, but they likely won't get there before sunrise."

Sam Gaskill was the Glacier Creek base captain, responsible for overseeing the operations of the ground crews, the aircrews, and the search and rescue crews. With the crazy wildfire season they'd been experiencing, Dylan knew the Glacier Creek base was short-staffed. Most of their crews were deployed to Oregon and California to help contain the massive wildfires there. Dylan had no idea how many firefighters remained at the Glacier Creek base, but suspected it might be just the part-timers and volunteers. Guys like himself. Christ, could it get any worse?

"How many crews have been deployed?"

"We've sent out two ground crews and we're getting air support and an additional crew from Idaho."

Dylan scrubbed a hand over his face. "What's the forecast?"

"Temperatures dropping into the fifties and winds increasing, but no rain in the forecast. I'm sorry, Dylan."

"Yeah, me too." He blew out a hard breath. "Okay. I'll get them to the Thunder Wolf Trail by sunrise."

"I know you will," Jacqui said. "Be careful, okay?"

Dylan switched off the handheld unit and stood with his head bowed for a minute, considering his options. The trek overland to the Thunder Wolf Trail would entail negotiating a narrow path along a sheer cliff, and crossing a deep ravine before they encountered the upper end of the Flat River where it intersected the Thunder Wolf Trail. A rope bridge traversed the deep river gorge, but once on the other side, Dylan thought they could pass the night in relative safety.

"Hey, is everything okay?"

Dylan raised his head to see Hayden had come to stand beside him. Concern clouded her blue eyes.

"Yeah," he said, forcing a smile. "Everything's great."

"Don't lie to me," she said, her glance flicking to where the others sat watching them. "It's bad, isn't it?"

Dylan searched her eyes for a moment, wondering how much he should tell her. Would she freak out, or cause the others to panic if he told her just how dire their situation was?

"It's bad," he finally said. "We can't stop here. We need to keep moving."

"How bad?"

"We now have two wildfires moving in on both sides of us. The first one is literally licking at our heels. We have a hell of a lot of backcountry to negotiate before we can consider ourselves out of danger."

"You need to tell the others," she said quietly. "I know you think they can't handle it, but they can. In fact, it could be the only way you manage to light a fire under their butts—no pun intended."

"We don't have a lot of time."

"Then you should talk fast."

Dylan nodded. "You're right. And for what it's worth, I'm sorry about all of this."

"Why?" Her voice held a note of astonishment. "None of this is your fault."

"Maybe not, but if I hadn't encouraged you to hike up to the falls, you and the boys might have turned back and been safely at the campground by now."

He saw by the expression on her face, she had expected him to say something about Jackson, and how he had likely started the wildfire. But now wasn't the time for that discussion. He figured there would be time to talk about that later.

"Or we could have been trapped by the wildfire, without anyone to help us," she countered. "But through a stroke of good luck we're with you, and you're going to get us to safety."

Dylan only hoped she was right. He gathered the group around him and spread his trail map out on the ground, showing them their current position, where the two fires were approaching from, and where they needed to hike to in order for rescue teams to extract them safely.

"I know this doesn't look like a huge distance on the map," he said, "but it's a twelve-mile hike across terrain that's pretty rugged, and we don't know what we might encounter."

"Bears?" Ollie asked, his blue eyes round.

Dylan looked at the boy. "Maybe. But they'll want to avoid us as much as we want to avoid them, so I don't want you to worry about that, okay?"

"Why are we wasting all this time hiking overland?" Wesley asked. "Shouldn't we just head to the summit? A helicopter will have a better chance of picking us up there, above the tree line, than it will in these woods. The forest is a death trap."

His sentiments were echoed by several of the teens. Even the two older women, Vicki and Gloria, nodded their agreement.

"Look at these lines, here," Dylan said, indicating the dozens of tiny, tight lines that intersected the Eagle's Bluff Trail where it extended beyond Eagle Rock. "This indicates a forty percent grade, and I promise you we cannot negotiate that steep of an incline, not with any speed."

"Speak for yourself," Wesley muttered.

Dylan sharpened his gaze on the other man, not bothering to hide his dislike. "Actually, I speak for everyone in this group." His gaze swept over each person in turn, and finally settled on Jackson and Ollie. "Each of you is my responsibility, per direction of the U.S. Forest Service. There is no cell phone reception out here. Right now, I'm you're only link to civilization and safety. If you want to survive this, you'll do exactly as I say."

"I'm coming with you!" This from a teenaged girl named Allie, who looked at him with something close to hero worship in her dark eyes. "And so are my friends."

Dylan gave each of the others a questioning look.

"We'll come with you," Gloria said, holding Vicki's hand.

"My son and I are with you," Richard said, even as he shot a quelling glance at Wesley. "And we won't slow you down."

"Okay, then, we should move." Dylan withdrew a compass from his pack and consulted it, before studying the forest above them. "This is where we leave the trail, and make our way cross country. I'm not going to lie to you; this isn't going to be easy."

Unexpectedly, Ollie burst into tears.

"Ollie, what is it?" Hayden asked, crouching in front of the little boy. "Are you okay?"

Ollie threw his arms around Hayden's neck and sobbed

harder.

"Shh," Hayden soothed, rubbing his back. "Everything will be fine, I promise."

Dylan suspected he was crying because he felt responsible for the wildfire.

Jackson scowled. "He's just trying to get attention."

"I am not!" Ollie flung himself away from Hayden and turned on his brother, his face red with rage and something else.

Clearly surprised, Jackson stepped back. "Then why are you crying?"

"You know why!" Ollie screamed, as tears streamed down his thin face. Then, as if overwhelmed by the emotions churning through him, he gave an impotent cry of sheer frustration, before he turned and stomped up the trail.

Hayden stood up and took Jackson by the arm, leading him away from the group. She bent and spoke to the older boy for a moment, and then released him. Dylan couldn't hear what she said, but when she let him go, Jackson walked over to where the teenagers stood together.

Hayden rejoined the group with a strained expression. "Ollie will walk with me, and Jackson can walk with the teenagers," she said to Dylan. "He's practically one himself, so he doesn't need to stay with me."

Dylan suspected she wanted to separate the boys, and provide Jackson with less opportunity to bully or belittle Ollie.

"Okay, listen up," he said, folding the map and pushing it into his pack. "I'm going to go first as we traverse the mountain, followed by Ollie and Hayden, Gloria and Vicki, the minors—" he spared a swift grin for the teenagers "—and then Richard and Wesley. I want each of you to keep your eyes open for anything—bears, wildfire, other hikers—whatever. Watch your step, and stay close."

They pushed their way through the forest, hugging the steep incline of the mountain, and occasionally adjusting their direction. They crossed several small streams, and when they emerged from the forest, there was a collective gasp of astonishment from everyone in the group.

Dylan had led them along the edge of the mountain, and now they stood on a high ridge overlooking a deep, heavily timbered valley. On the far side, rose another line of mountains. Flames licked along the base of those mountains, and the dense pine forest on the valley floor was shrouded in thick, white mist, and only the tops of the conifers were visible.

Only it wasn't mist—it was smoke.

The sight was both horrifying and eerily beautiful.

They'd heard the churning, thwap-thwap-thwap of a helicopter as they'd made their way through the forest, and now they could see the chopper as it flew overhead, assessing the fire.

"Oh my God," Hayden breathed, as she came to stand beside him. "We were just there."

"Hey," said one of the teen boys. Dylan recalled his name was Ryan. "Why can't that helicopter lift us out of here?"

"It's not equipped to carry more than a couple of people," Dylan replied. "Even if it could, there's no safe place for it to touch down."

"Maybe they could hoist us in a basket, like they do in the movies." This from one of the girls, Kendra, who hugged her towel around her shoulders. "I just want to go home."

"Are you sure you know where you're going?" Richard asked.

"Absolutely," Dylan said.

"But is it safe?" asked Vicki. "Those fires look closer than I'd like."

"We're safe as long as we keep moving, and as long as we stay together."

But as they continued to make their way slowly along the steep ridge, everyone's eyes were on the fire, and Dylan knew they were all thinking the same thing: *Could he really save them?*

Chapter Six

WHEN DARKNESS CAME, it descended so quickly Hayden was hardly aware of the loss of light. She only knew one moment she could see the ground, and the next moment she was stumbling as her eyes adjusted to the lack of depth perception.

Behind her, Ollie stumbled, too. She reached behind her and found his hand. "You okay, bud?"

"Yeah," he said, but his voice sound thin and reedy.

They'd been hiking for what seemed like hours. She thought of the snug little Airstream trailer parked at the Glacier Creek campground. Were the other campers aware of the wildfire, or that there were hikers trapped above the fire line?

Glancing behind her, she saw that the others in the group appeared as dark, shapeless shadows. Several of the teens used their cell phones to illuminate the path, and the lights bobbed in the darkness like bright fireflies. There was very little talking. Everyone was tired, and the bright orange glow on the far mountain ridge was a constant reminder that the wildfires weren't so distant.

"Okay, let's do a headcount," Dylan called, and brought the group to a halt.

He'd done the same thing about every thirty minutes, and Hayden knew he was concerned about the group and of letting anyone fall behind, especially now that it was dark. They'd already crossed a deep gorge, where the steep embankments had been made of loose, rolling rocks. Gloria had tripped and then slid almost all the way to the bottom. When they'd finally reached her side, she'd been bleeding from numerous cuts and scrapes, but luckily hadn't seriously injured herself.

Dylan had pulled out a first aid packet and proceeded to tend to Gloria's injuries, as Hayden talked with the older woman in an attempt to distract her.

Hayden understood how she'd fallen; the skies to the south had glowed with an eerie, orange light that alternately grew brighter, and then dimmed. They'd all been mesmerized by the sight. Against the darkening sky, the enormity of the encroaching wildfire had been frightening. With the steep, unstable embankment, it was no wonder Gloria had fallen. Hayden had almost lost her own footing, staring at the unnatural glow.

Now Dylan stopped briefly in front of her. She couldn't see his face, but his large bulk was a reassuring presence in the darkness.

"You doing okay?" he asked quietly.

"We're good," she assured him.

"How are you doing, little man?" he asked Ollie.

"Okay." Ollie had been uncharacteristically quiet during the long hike, and even Hayden's attempts to draw him into conversation had been met with one-word answers.

Dylan moved down the length of the line, tapping each person's arm as he counted off. Satisfied they still numbered thirteen, he spent an extra few minutes with Gloria, checking on her injuries and making sure she felt well enough to continue.

He strode back to the front of the group, and stopped next to Hayden. "Take a few minutes and have something to drink," he suggested. "I'm going to radio in and let them know our position, and see if there's a plan to drop supplies in."

Some blankets at the very least, Hayden thought, shivering.

Dylan stepped away from the group and turned on the two-way radio. The static squawk startled Ollie, and he pressed closer to Hayden. As she pulled a water bottle out of her pack, she could hear the conversation, although it was difficult to make out some of the responses to Dylan's questions.

When he finally ended the call, he turned to the group. "The U.S. Forest Service is sending a ranger in from the other direction to meet us with blankets and food," he said. "We're almost there, so don't give up. You're all doing great!"

A small cheer went up as he delivered this welcome news.

"I hope they bring Thermoses of hot chocolate," Allie said.

"And s'mores," Kendra replied, laughing.

Dylan stepped close to Hayden, and she could feel the rampant heat radiating from his big body, as if the rapidly dropping temperature was no match for the excess energy he contained.

"I hope the kids aren't too disappointed when the ranger brings Mylar blankets and energy bars," Dylan said drily.

"I don't think anyone will complain," Hayden said. Now that they had stopped, she couldn't seem to control her shivering. "I know I won't. How much further do we need to go tonight?"

"Thunder Wolf Trail is just a few miles ahead. We'll need to cross over the Flat River, but there's a rope bridge we can use. Once we're on the other side of the river, we'll follow it upstream to Angel Falls, and camp there for the night."

"Okay, that sounds g-good."

"Hey, you're cold." He stepped closer and rubbed her bare arms briskly with his big, warm hands. "Your skin is chilled."

"I'm fine," she assured him, wishing he didn't have to stop. "Really. Some of the girls are only wearing their bathing suits. At least I have a shirt on."

The temperatures had slowly started to drop with the

setting sun, an irony that wasn't lost on the group, as they watched unholy orange flames consume a distant ridge of trees. On the far side of the valley, where they had been just hours earlier, the entire mountainside burned brightly. Even where they stood, the air was smoky and acrid.

Hayden had packed sweatshirts for herself and the boys, but had given hers to one of the girls, after noticing her lips were turning blue. Dylan had done the same, handing over a zip-up fleece and an extra T-shirt to the other two girls.

"Let's keep moving, then," he said now. "The exercise will help keep you warm."

They reached the Thunder Wolf Trail two hours later, and a whoop went up from the teenagers. But when they reached the swinging rope bridge that would take them over the river, even the teenagers faltered. Hayden didn't blame them; she wasn't certain she wanted to cross the insubstantial bridge. Constructed of rope handles and a wooden plank base, it extended across a deep gorge. Hayden couldn't see the water, but she could hear it tumbling over the rocks in the darkness far below.

"Why do we have to cross this rickety old thing?" Wesley demanded. "Why can't we hike along the river on this side?"

"Because the trail is on the other side," Dylan explained patiently. "If we don't cross here, we don't cross at all."

Wesley made a dismissive sound, as if the explanation didn't answer his question, but he thankfully didn't pursue it.

"I want you to go first," Dylan said quietly to Hayden. "The boys trust you. If they see you cross over safely, they'll go, too. If the three of you cross, then the rest will do it."

"I don't know," she began uncertainly. "How long is it?"

"About eighty feet across."

Tentatively, Hayden put her hands on the rope rails, but stepped quickly back when she felt them give beneath her weight. "I can't see the other side," she protested. "How do I know it's connected?"

"Allie," he called. "Bring me your phone."

Allie came forward and handed him her cell phone. Dylan switched on the flashlight app and aimed it at the bridge. But instead of reassuring her, the sight made Hayden's knees turn to water. The bridge dipped in the middle, before swinging upward again to the far side, where it disappeared into the darkness. It looked impossibly narrow, and far too fragile to support the weight of one person, never mind fourteen.

"I can't do it," she whispered, and took another step backward.

"Hey, come here," Dylan said, and pulled her swiftly into his arms. He was so big, and so impossibly warm, that Hayden's first instinct was to burrow into him. All too soon, he set her free. "It's okay, I have a better idea."

With Allie's phone in his hand, he stepped onto the bridge, and the light bobbed up and down as he made his way across.

Hayden held her breath.

After a moment, the light dipped down and stopped moving. Then Dylan was back, a big shadow materializing from the darkness of the gorge. Hayden realized she had been holding her breath, and she blew it out in a rush of relief. On the far side, the cell phone glowed like a beacon where he'd left it.

"The bridge is connected, and it's perfectly safe." She could hear the smile in his voice. "All you have to do is hold on to the sides, and walk directly toward the light."

"Why does that sound suspiciously like dying?" she muttered, but Dylan only laughed softly.

"I promise you, I will not let that happen." He turned to the group. "Who's going to go first?"

"I'll go," Ryan offered, stepping forward.

"Good man," Dylan said approvingly.

Ryan stepped onto the bridge. "No problem!" he called back to them. "It's a little bouncy, but it doesn't swing side to side. I'm on the other side! There's a nice flat space over here, and I can see where the trail heads down."

Hayden couldn't see him, but when he picked up the cell phone and waved the light in an arc, the group let out a cheer and clapped. After that, the teenagers were anxious to join him, and although there were several squeals of fright as they walked across, they each made it safely to the opposite side of the gorge. Even Jackson went across, and Hayden smiled as she heard the older girls praising him for being so brave. Vicki and Gloria went next, and then Richard.

Finally, it was just Dylan, Hayden, Ollie and Wesley.

"Who's next?" Dylan asked. "Ollie, why don't you go with me?"

"Yeah, okay," Ollie said, and there was no mistaking the relief in his voice.

"I'll go next," Hayden volunteered, even as her stomach clenched in dread. "I'll see you on the other side, Ollie."

"You'll do fine," Dylan assured her. "Just keep your eyes on the light."

Hayden nodded. Drawing a deep breath, she stepped onto the bridge, feeling the planks dip beneath her weight. The rope handles were rough beneath her fingers, and she clung to them with a fierce determination as she took another step, and then another.

"This is terrifying!" she called over her shoulder to Dylan.

Suddenly, the bridge gave an alarming lurch and Hayden let out a surprised cry, clutching the ropes as she struggled to maintain her balance.

"Wesley, what the hell are you doing?" Dylan shouted. "The bridge isn't designed for two people to cross at the same time!"

"The lady is frightened," Wesley retorted. "I'll go across with her."

"No, Wesley!" Hayden cried, gripping the ropes, even as the bridge bounced beneath her feet. "You're making it tip!

It isn't safe! Please go back!"

"It's okay," he panted, directly in her ear. His breath was fast and hot. "I'm right here, and I won't let anything happen to you."

His arm snaked around her waist, and only the fear of falling kept Hayden from shoving him away. As it was, the planks dipped and rose sickeningly beneath their combined weight.

"Let me go," she gasped. "I don't need your help."

He pressed against her, making her grateful for the backpack she wore. "Don't be afraid. I'll help you."

Suddenly, his arm was gone. The ropes and planks wobbled as Dylan pulled him back off the bridge, ignoring the other man's angry protests.

"Go ahead, Hayden," Dylan called. "You're fine."

With her heart pounding hard in her chest, Hayden kept her eyes on the cell phone light and focused on putting one foot in front of the other, blocking out the encouraging shouts from the teenagers on the far side. Finally, she reached the opposite side, and Jackson flung his arms around her waist.

"You did it!"

She hugged him, and dragged in a couple of calming breaths. "Thanks, bud." She wasn't sure she would have had the courage to cross the bridge if she'd been able to look down and see the distance to the water, below. Now she turned and peered through the darkness to where Dylan remained with Ollie.

"I made it!" she called out.

A dark shape materialized out of the gloom, and Wesley stepped from the bridge.

"Good job," he muttered as he shoved past her, deliberately pushing her off-balance, and his tone lacked any real warmth.

Hayden caught his arm, forcing him to stop. "What were you thinking?" she demanded. "You could have made me fall or, worse, the bridge could have broken beneath our weight!"

"I was just trying to help," he said, his tone sullen and defensive. "Trust me, I won't make that mistake again. You two deserve each other."

Shaking off her hand, he retreated toward the edge of the group, while Hayden watched in open-mouthed dismay. Finally, she turned back to the bridge. She could hear the creaking of the ropes and knew Dylan was on his way across. When she could finally make out his shape, it was to see he carried Ollie piggyback style, with his backpack secured against his chest. He set the boy down when he reached Hayden, and gave Ollie a high five.

"Good job, little man," he said, swinging his pack over his shoulder. He turned to Hayden and she could feel his scrutiny even in the darkness. "Are you okay? Did he hurt you?"

"No, I'm fine." She turned and glanced toward the spot where Wesley stood talking with Gloria, Vicki, and Richard.

"I think he meant well, but I could feel the bridge moving and it just freaked me out."

Dylan made a sound of disgust. "He was out of line. I'm sorry I didn't stop him in time."

"It wasn't your fault," she assured him. "We all made it across, and that's the important thing."

Dylan turned and looked across the gorge to the ridge they had just hiked across. Beyond the ghostly silhouette of the trees, the sky blazed in hues of orange and red.

"Is it getting closer?" Hayden asked. "Will it reach this far?"

"Hard to say from this distance," Dylan muttered. "But the firefighting base would have contacted me if we were in any immediate danger. The Forest Service knows our position."

"Hopefully we'll be out of here soon," she replied, hugging her arms around her middle.

"You're cold," Dylan said.

"Getting there," she admitted.

"We're almost to the spot where we can spend the night," he said. "Once we're there, I'll get you warm."

The images that swamped Hayden's imagination were so graphically sexual that heat suffused her entire body. She had no business thinking about him that way, not under their present circumstances. Flustered by the direction of her thoughts, she stepped away from him and took Ollie's hand.

"Then we should get going," she said.

THEY CAMPED FOR the night on a dirt-packed embankment near a small waterfall. Dylan stepped away to speak into his radio. Hayden hoped he was right, and that a ranger from the U.S. Forest Service would soon arrive with emergency blankets and food. The teenagers were huddled on the ground about ten feet away, wrapped in their towels as they tried to stay warm. Hayden was grateful she'd thought to pack a sweatshirt for each of the boys, but they still shivered as the temperature continued to drop.

"I'm starving," Jackson complained. "Do you have any more food?"

"I packed some extra sandwiches, so you can share one," Hayden said. "We'll save the last sandwich for the morning, just in case."

"Just in case…what?" Ollie asked.

Just in case the ranger didn't arrive.

Dylan strode back into the center of the group and slid his backpack off. "I'm sorry, but I don't have good news," he said now. "The ranger they sent to meet us was detoured to help another group of hikers trapped by the wildfires. We're on our own until morning, but I don't want anyone to worry. We'll be fine."

"Why do other hikers get priority over us?" Wesley asked in dismay. "We have women and children in our group. Doesn't that mean anything?"

"The other group had a pregnant woman and a two-year old child," Dylan said quietly. "They needed help getting to an area where they could be safely airlifted out."

There was silence as the group considered his words.

"Okay, let's everyone pull out any food, water and extra clothing," Dylan directed. "If you have anything you can spare, please share it with the minors, since they didn't come prepared for an overnight hike."

Dylan bent over his own pack and began pulling items out. The first was a small, cylindrical light, which he switched on. There was an immediate murmur of appreciation, and the group drew closer to the bright circle of light, anxious to keep the surrounding darkness at bay. He withdrew a waterproof packet of energy bars, which he tossed to the teenagers, and two thermal blankets. He handed one to Hayden, and the other to Gloria and Vicki.

"But what about you?" Hayden asked, as she unfolded the thin, Mylar blanket and tucked it around the boys.

"I'm fine," he assured her. He nodded toward her pack. "What do you have in there?"

Hayden opened her backpack and began withdrawing items. She didn't have much. There were two bottles of water, the two sandwiches, a zip-lock bag of sliced apples and another of orange wedges, and a carton of chocolate covered malted milk balls. Now she spread them out on top of her backpack for Dylan's inspection.

"I promised the boys they could share a sandwich now

and save the other one for the morning, but if anyone would like the fruit and chocolate, they're welcome to it," she said.

In the end, they pooled enough food to ensure everyone had something to eat. Dylan directed the teenagers to huddle together for the night in order to share and conserve warmth, while Gloria and Vicki did the same. Richard and Wesley sat shoulder to shoulder against a large tree trunk. Wesley had their swim towels spread over their legs, and they each wore a fleece jacket.

Hayden sat on the ground with her back against the hard-packed embankment. Ollie had curled himself into a small ball on her lap and had fallen asleep almost instantly. She guessed he was both physically and emotionally drained, and her heart ached for him. Pulling the Mylar blanket around them, she kept one arm protectively around Ollie, while she hugged Jackson against her side with her free arm. She'd been surprised and pleased when he'd opted to stay with her for the night, rather than the teenagers. Now he shivered slightly, and she pressed him closer. Beneath her fingers, his shoulder blades were thin and sharp, reminding her he was still young, despite his surly attitude.

"I'm sorry, Auntie Hayden," he whispered now.

"What are you sorry for, bud?"

He was silent for a long moment, and when he finally spoke his voice was muffled against her sweatshirt. "I did start the fire."

Hayden closed her eyes and drew in a deep, calming

breath. "How do you know?" she whispered. "You said they all went out before they hit the ground."

"They did, and I stepped on them to make sure. But…" His voice trailed off.

"But what?"

"But then we heard Dylan say something about a bear, and we got scared. I dropped the last match, and I think it was still lit. But I'm not sure! Ollie took off running, and I ran too. I don't remember stepping on the last match."

"Oh, Jackson," she said softly, and bent to press a kiss against his soft hair. He smelled like pine sap and sunscreen, but overlaying those wonderful boy smells was the unmistakable odor of acrid smoke. "Why didn't you say something?"

"I was too scared." He paused. "What's going to happen to me?"

Hayden hugged him closer and rested her chin on his head. "We'll just explain what happened, and that it was an accident."

Jackson looked uncertain. "But is it an accident if I was throwing the matches on the ground?"

"Why did you take them?" Hayden asked softly. "You must have known I wouldn't approve."

Jackson shrugged. "I don't know. I see Dad doing it all the time. I guess I just wanted to try it." He looked up at Hayden with brimming eyes. "I'm sorry, Auntie Hayden. I'll never do it again."

Hayden closed her eyes briefly. She could hear the fear

and anxiety in Jackson's voice, and desperately wanted to reassure him that there would be no consequences for him, but she knew that would be a lie. She'd gone through a similar experience when she was fourteen, and she only hoped the boys wouldn't have to suffer the way she had. Whatever happened, she wouldn't abandon them. She'd stand by them, no matter what. She would need to contact Molly as soon as possible, to explain what had happened. Whatever her relationship with her sister, she trusted Molly to know what to do.

"I know you didn't mean for the fire to start," she finally said. "I don't want to lecture you, but I hope you understand just how dangerous playing with matches can be." She gave him a squeeze. "Sometimes we adults tell you not to do something because it's for your own safety, and not because we want to make your life your miserable. But whatever happens, I'm going to be right there with you. No matter what. Okay?"

Jackson nodded. "Okay."

Dylan came to sit beside Hayden, moving close in order to share his warmth.

"Here, let me take Ollie," he said. "He's almost as big as you."

Dylan lifted the sleeping child from Hayden's lap and settled him instead against his own chest. Then he put an arm around Hayden and snugged her up against his side. He seemed impervious to the falling temperatures, and she was grateful for his warmth, and the security he represented.

He kept the small light on throughout the night, and Hayden was pretty sure none of them slept. She could see the glow of the wildfire in the distance, and couldn't help but watch as it grew brighter and then faded, and then grew brighter again.

On the other side of the clearing, the teenagers lay huddled together on the ground, sharing the blanket and towels. They whispered quietly amongst themselves. Jackson leaned heavily against Hayden's side and fell into a fitful sleep, while Ollie slept in the crook of Dylan's arm. Once, during the night, Hayden heard something moving in the woods behind them—something big, and so close she could actually hear its breath puffing in and out. Her heart rate quickened. Reaching over, she sought Dylan's hand, gratified when his strong fingers closed around hers.

"Bear," he mouthed silently to her, then in a whisper, "Don't worry, it'll keep moving. It's not interested in us."

Sure enough, the noises slowly grew more distant, and then the surrounding forest was silent. Dylan didn't release her hand. Instead, he kept it loosely clasped in his own, and absently stroked his thumb over her skin. Hayden was grateful for the reassuring contact. Her head rested in the curve of his shoulder, and she listened to the even rhythm of his breathing. He radiated heat, and Hayden felt a flicker of guilt that she was likely warmer than the others in their small group. She had to resist the urge to nestle even closer, reminding herself she didn't know Dylan well enough, but wishing she could change that.

She watched the flickering orange sky, and her thoughts returned to what Jackson had confessed to her. He was the reason the entire mountainside was burning. He'd admitted to playing with the matches, and possibly allowing a lit one to land unchecked on the dry forest floor. She glanced down at him. His lashes were long and dark against his pale cheeks, and his mouth was slack in sleep. He looked so young and vulnerable, that her heart ached.

Her arm tightened reflexively around Jackson. Whatever happened, she wouldn't abandon him the way her own family had abandoned her.

Chapter Seven

THE FOLLOWING MORNING, after a chilly, sleepless night, they hiked out of the mountains and were met on a fire road by two men from the U.S. Forest Service. They provided the weary group with food and blankets, and drove them back to the original trailhead, where most of them had left a vehicle.

During the ride, Hayden let her mind wander back to that morning. She'd fallen into a fitful sleep, with Jackson's head pillowed on her lap. But when she'd woken up, her own head had been pillowed on Dylan's chest, and he'd had his arm around her. In the hazy predawn darkness, the boys had been sound asleep on either side of them, and when she tipped her head, it was to find herself looking directly into Dylan's warm, amber-flecked gaze.

"Hey," he'd murmured softly.

"Hey." She'd stared at him in sleepy bemusement for a moment, and then he'd bent his head down and kissed her. It had been no more than a brief, soft fusing of his warm lips against hers, but it had thrown her completely off-balance. She didn't need the kind of complication he represented, and yet everything in her had ached for his touch. She'd dragged her mouth away from his and scrambled away from him, waking Jackson up in the process. She'd been unable to meet Dylan's gaze for most of the remaining hike, and had chalked her shaky legs and light-headedness up to the unexpected kiss.

Now she listened in growing unease as Dylan talked to the other men about the wildfire, and the damage it had caused. Aside from the hundreds of acres of burned forest, the wildfire had forced the evacuation of several homes, and had destroyed a local lumber mill.

As they pulled into the small parking lot where she and the boys had begun their hike the day before, Hayden saw the air was smoky, even down here. Teary family members were already there to meet the teenagers, and an ambulance stood nearby with two EMTs to evaluate anyone who required medical care. Hayden was disconcerted to see several television news vans parked in the small lot, and a group of reporters and cameramen waiting to talk to the hikers.

Hayden held the boys back, and allowed everyone else to exit the small bus first. Only when the reporters were engaged in talking to the teens and to Richard and Wesley, did she hustle the boys out of the bus. The last thing she wanted was to be interviewed for the six o'clock news. When one reporter approached, she held up a hand and walked faster, keeping her face averted.

"No comment," she said, and waved them away.

She just wanted to return to the Airstream, take a hot shower, and sleep. She'd been nursing a headache since she'd woken up, and her legs felt wobbly and weak, probably from the unaccustomed activity. She was herding Jackson and Ollie toward the Jeep when Dylan fell into step beside her.

"Sure you're okay?" he asked.

"Yes, positive," she assured him. "I really just want to get back to the campground and get the boys showered and fed."

"Sure, I understand." He paused. "Listen, can I talk to you?"

Hayden looked at her two nephews. "Boys, go wait for me in the Jeep, please." When they were out of earshot, she turned to Dylan. "What is it?"

Dylan thrust his hands into his front pockets and scrutinized her through narrowed eyes. "You know I have to report what I saw, what I know, to the authorities, right?"

Hayden felt the skin on the back of her neck tighten. She glanced past him to where the news crews were looking around for fresh victims.

"Can you do me a favor?" she asked quietly. "Let me tell the authorities."

Dylan's expression was both compassionate and resigned. "When?"

Hayden glanced toward the Jeep. "Either later today, or tomorrow at the latest. We're all exhausted and dirty. Waiting one day isn't going to make any difference, is it? I'd rather not subject the boys to a grueling interrogation when they've been through so much."

"Okay," he finally said, and rubbed one hand across the back of his neck. "They're going to ask me what I know, but I'll stall for as long as I can."

"Thank you," she said with heartfelt appreciation. "Maybe the investigation will show the boys had nothing to do with the fire. Maybe it began through natural causes."

"Maybe it did and maybe it didn't," he said gently. "All I'm saying is, I can be the one to tell the investigators what I know—or you can."

Hayden felt a little ill, both at the knowledge of what might happen to the boys, and the realization that Dylan didn't completely trust her to do the right thing.

"I'll tell them everything," she assured him. "I just want to let the boys get some food and sleep first."

"They're not going to toss the boys in jail or remove them from your care, if that's what you're worried about," Dylan said.

Hayden felt the earth suddenly tilt sideways on its axis, and for just an instant the ground reeled beneath her feet. The headache that had nagged her since dawn was now a wrecking ball. She felt light-headed and nauseous, and blackness fluttered at the edge of her vision. She flung out a hand, but Dylan was already there, catching her in his arms as her knees buckled and she began to go down.

"I need a medic!" he shouted over his shoulder, as he

lowered her to the ground.

"No," Hayden tried to protest, "I'm okay." But the world was still spinning, and she felt like she might be sick at any moment.

"Shh. Let them take a look," Dylan said soothingly. "This is why they're here."

Before she could push herself out of Dylan's embrace, two EMTs were bending over her, looking at her pupils and taking her blood pressure with their blue-gloved hands.

"When's the last time you ate, ma'am?" the first medic asked.

"I—I can't remember," she replied.

"Did you eat anything this morning?" Dylan asked.

"She didn't eat anything this morning, or last night!" Jackson said.

Hayden looked up to see both boys standing over them, their faces tight and anxious.

"I told you…wait in the Jeep," she managed to say.

Dylan tightened his hold on her. "You haven't had anything to eat since lunch, yesterday? Why?"

Hayden heard the disbelief and anger in his voice. "The boys were hungry," she said. "They needed it more."

The first medic, who had been checking her pulse, looked at her. "You're clammy and your heart rate is accelerated. You're likely suffering from dehydration. Why don't you come to the hospital for intravenous fluids?"

"No," she protested, and struggled to sit up, pushing

Dylan away. "I just had a moment, but I'm fine now."

"You're not fine," Dylan said, his voice grim. "You're stubborn. Go with them, and I'll follow right behind you with the boys. We'll meet you there."

Hayden nodded, mortified to feel hot tears well up. She didn't have the strength to resist when Dylan helped her to her feet and all but carried her over to the ambulance, where she was helped onto a gurney and lifted into the back of the vehicle. The reporters, with their news cameras and lights, swarmed around them, and Hayden covered her face with her hands. This couldn't be happening.

Not again.

Dylan climbed into the ambulance and bent over her. "Don't worry about anything," he said. His expression was both tender and concerned. "We'll meet you at the hospital, okay?"

Too choked to respond, she simply nodded. Dylan squeezed her hand, and climbed out of the vehicle. An EMT sat beside her, preparing an IV drip. She raised her head to see Dylan standing in the parking lot with the boys, and then someone closed the doors to the ambulance, and they were gone.

AT THE HOSPITAL, Hayden found herself in the emergency room, hooked to an IV, while a nurse brought her drinks and snacks. As good as his word, Dylan and the boys arrived shortly after she'd been settled in. He brought her a cheeseburger, fries, and a large lemonade.

"Oh, that smells incredible," she moaned, digging into the food. "But what about you guys?"

"We ate ours on the way over," Jackson said. "Dylan ate two burgers!"

"We picked them up at a little shack by the town pier," Dylan said. "They are hands down the best burgers in town."

Hayden could only nod in agreement, as she chewed in bliss. The burger was, indeed, the best she'd ever eaten. But as hungry as she was, she could only manage half, before pushing it away with a sigh of contentment.

"Thank you," she said to Dylan. "That was delicious. I'm actually starting to feel better."

"Do you have to stay here all day?" Ollie asked, as he sat on the end of the hospital bed.

"No," she assured him. "As soon as this bag of fluids is gone, we can leave. Okay?"

"Okay."

"Is that what the doctor said?" Dylan asked, suspicion lurking in his eyes.

"It's what I said," she replied firmly. "I'm fine, really. I already feel better."

"I'm glad to hear it." He pushed his hands into the front pockets of his shorts and hunched his shoulders. "So, uh, I guess I'll head out. Your Jeep is just outside in the visitor's lot, and the keys are in your backpack."

"Oh. Okay, sure."

Hayden didn't know why his words surprised her. After all, he had no obligation toward her or the boys, and there was no reason for him to hang around at the hospital. They barely knew each other. She had no right to feel like he was ditching her. Hadn't she just assured him she was fine? That she could leave the hospital just as soon as the fluids were gone? So why did she feel so deflated by the news that he wasn't going to stick around?

"Hey, boys." Dylan pulled out his wallet and handed several one-dollar bills to Jackson. "I think I saw a vending machine down the hallway. Think you could find something in there you like?"

"Yes!" Ollie snatched the money from Jackson's hand and bolted from the room.

Jackson hung back. "Is this your way of trying to get rid of us?"

"Just for a couple of minutes," Dylan admitted. "I need to talk to your aunt. Deal?" He reached out for a fist-bump, and after an initial hesitation, Jackson bumped him.

"Deal," he said. "But only a few minutes. I don't know how long I can keep Ollie busy."

He left, and Dylan raked a hand through his hair. Hayden pushed herself higher up against the pillows. "What is it?" she asked, before he could say anything.

She was unprepared when he perched himself on the

edge of the narrow mattress. His hip pressed against hers, and there was nowhere for her to go. No escape.

"We need to figure out how we're going to handle this," he said, his expression so compassionate Hayden felt tears threaten. "You don't need to do this by yourself."

She didn't pretend to misunderstand him. "Thank you," she said. "But how can I be sure the boys won't face charges, or be sent away?"

"That won't happen," Dylan said. "They'll be remanded to the custody of their parents, and I have to think the authorities will go easy on them because of their age."

"But you don't know for sure," Hayden persisted, searching his face. "What if you're wrong? Sometimes, the world doesn't care if they're just kids."

Dylan gave her a quizzical look. "Am I missing something?"

"I'm just saying you can't make any guarantees," Hayden said, not meeting his eyes.

He put a hand over hers, enclosing her fingers in the warm strength of his own. "Listen to me. I've been battling wildfires for a long time, all over the country. Some of those blazes were ignited by kids not much older than Jackson, and I promise you, none of them went to jail or juvie." He tipped his head down to look directly into her eyes. "It will be okay."

Hayden felt a betraying tightness in her throat, and knew she was in danger of becoming emotional—again. She blamed it on Dylan, and his sympathetic bedside manner.

"I blame myself more than I do the boys," she admitted. "I should never have had those matches in the first aid kit. I should have watched them more closely." She pressed her hands together. "My sister is never going to forgive me for this. Could you hand me my cell phone? I need to let her know what happened before she sees it on the evening news."

Dylan handed her the phone and stood up. "I'm going to head home and take a quick shower, but if you'd like, I'll come back and drive you and the boys to the campground."

"You don't need to do that," Hayden assured him, even as relief swirled through her. *He wasn't abandoning her.* "I can drive."

Dylan stood up, amusement creasing his eyes. "So stubborn. I'll see you in an hour or so."

After he left, Hayden turned her phone on and then groaned when she realized the battery was completely dead. The IV drip was almost empty, and the doctor had assured her that as soon as the fluid was gone, she could leave. Physically, she felt fine. Emotionally, she'd never felt so conflicted in her life.

Chapter Eight

DYLAN DROVE TO his house on autopilot, so deep in thought he hardly registered passing through the downtown area of Glacier Creek. He took no notice of the summer tourists who strolled along the sidewalks and enjoyed the lake, despite the haze of smoke hanging in the air. All he could see was Hayden's pale face as she'd crumpled toward the ground, and how fragile she'd felt in his arms as he'd caught her.

He didn't want to feel any responsibility toward her. He wanted to walk away, and not get involved in her dilemma. He didn't want to care about what might happen to her, or the boys.

But he did, damn it. And that was the problem.

Where Hayden Temple was concerned, he'd lost any ability to make good decisions. Like kissing her this morning. He recalled again the soft sweetness of her lips, and the dreamy expression in her blue eyes when she opened them, just before reality had intruded and she'd realized where she was. He hadn't been able to help himself. Kissing her had been a biological imperative.

He had promised he would stall and not reveal what he knew about the wildfire, but that promise didn't sit well with him. He had seen the conflict in Hayden's eyes, and knew she was on the fence about telling the investigation team the truth. He understood Hayden's concerns, but if she didn't do the right thing and tell the authorities how the wildfire had started, then he'd have no choice but to tell them himself.

He hoped it wouldn't come to that.

Outside of town, he turned onto the road that led upward into the dense, forest-covered foothills behind Glacier Creek. He passed Laurel Cavanaugh's log house, and saw her VW Beetle parked in the driveway, which meant he could expect her to come knocking on his door precisely ten minutes after he got home.

The bestselling author of a popular mystery series, Laurel lived by herself and rarely ventured into town. Dylan guessed she was around thirty years old, and she was attractive in a shy, bookish way. Dylan knew she had a little bit of a crush on him, so he did his best not to send any signals that might raise her hopes. He liked her, but she wasn't his type, and he definitely wasn't in the market for a girlfriend—or a wife.

That made his thoughts return to Hayden Temple.

He kept telling himself she wasn't his type either, but he couldn't seem to stop thinking about her. There was something both fierce and vulnerable about her. He liked her spirit and her independence, and the way she loved her nephews. He only hoped Hayden wouldn't be held responsible for the wildfire; the U.S. Forest Service could levy charges of negligence. They could charge her for the cost of the wildfire containment efforts. Hopefully, when they learned the boys were responsible, they would go easy on them.

Unlocking the door to his timber-framed house, he stepped inside and dropped his backpack on a bench. Boomer, his enormous cat, strolled out of the kitchen and pushed his head against Dylan's leg with a loud meow.

"Hey, big guy," he said, "how're you doing?"

He'd found the cat a couple of years earlier, scavenging in the dumpster behind the firefighting base. He'd been thin, and his long coat had been matted and dirty. He'd been covered with ticks, and had several deep cuts on his face, as if he'd gone nose to nose with a badger. But when Dylan had picked him up, he'd purred with pleasure. Dylan had brought him to the vet, and when nobody had come forward to claim him, he'd brought him home. He was a big brown and black cat with six toes on each paw, and a ruff of fur around his neck that reminded Dylan of a lion's mane. With his tufted ears and permanent scowl, he looked downright unfriendly. But Dylan knew differently. Boomer loved attention, and would purr at the smallest gesture of affection.

"You hungry, pal?" he asked, as the cat followed him into the kitchen and wound himself around Dylan's legs.

Dylan opened a can of cat food and dumped it on a plate. He was just setting the dish on the floor when the doorbell rang.

"Ten minutes, on the dot," he said to the cat, and then louder, "C'mon in, door's open!"

Laurel came into the kitchen, carrying a baking pan.

"Hi Dylan," she said, staring at him through thick, black-rimmed glasses. "I saw your car drive past, and just wanted to bring you these." She set a pan of brownies down on the island.

"Thanks," Dylan said.

"I was, uh, worried about you," she continued, shifting awkwardly from one foot to the other. "What with the wildfire, and you hiking overnight. Are you okay?"

"Sure," he said. "I'm fine, but I'm not really fit company right now. I'm dirty, and I probably don't smell very good."

He saw Laurel's eyes widen behind the thick glasses, and then color seeped into her neck. "Of course. You probably want to take a shower and get some rest."

"Well, definitely take a shower."

"Maybe I could come over later?" she asked. "I made a casserole, and I could heat it up for dinner. I know you're probably tired, and I thought maybe you wouldn't want to cook for yourself."

"Thanks, but I have a friend at the hospital, and I promised her I would come back to help discharge her."

He could almost see Laurel's antennae go up. "Her?"

"Yeah." He scrubbed a hand over his face, reminding himself he didn't owe Laurel any explanations. Sure, she was a good neighbor, and she'd taken care of Boomer on numerous occasions when he'd been away for extended periods of time, but he'd never so much as looked at Laurel in a romantic or sexual way. "She was trapped by the wildfire, too, so I helped her and her two young nephews make it down safely, but she was taken to the hospital to be treated for dehydration and exhaustion."

"Is that the woman I saw on the news? The one who fainted in your arms?"

Dylan sharpened his gaze on her. "They showed that on the news?"

"Well, it's a big story! Every news station is covering it, literally on every channel." Laurel paused. "Doesn't that woman have a husband or someone who can help her?"

"No, actually. Listen, Laurel, I appreciate the brownies, but you don't need to come over and check on me. I'm not even sure I'm going to be around for dinner."

"Oh." Her tone sounded both surprised and hurt. "Well, I just wanted to be sure you were okay."

"And I am." He walked around her, toward the open door. He knew he was acting like a dick, but he didn't want to talk about Hayden Temple. Not with Laurel. "Thanks for coming over, but I really need to take that shower and head back to the hospital."

"Okay, I understand." Laurel bowed her head and walked past him. "I hope your friend is better."

After she was gone, Dylan strode into the living room

and flipped on the television. Sure enough, footage of the wildfire aired on every local channel. He paused when he saw himself at the trailhead, catching Hayden in his arms as her knees buckled. EMTs and reporters swarmed around them, before the footage switched to an aerial view of the wildfire. Until that moment, Dylan hadn't had a good appreciation for just how widespread the devastation was. When they showed the Holliday family lumber mill in charred ruins, he felt his gut clench. The coverage switched to an interview between Sam Gaskill and a reporter, and Dylan turned the volume up.

"Captain Gaskill, how and where did the blaze start?" the reporter asked. Behind them, black smoke filled the horizon.

Sam, dressed in his full wildland firefighting gear, looked tired and grim. His face was streaked with soot, and his eyes were red-rimmed from the smoke and heat.

"There's an ongoing investigation into the origins of the wildfire," he said, "but it appears the Flat River blaze started somewhere along the Larch Trail or the lower Eagle's Bluff Trail. We have investigators scouring the area now for any indication of what may have sparked that blaze. The second fire, which appears to have ignited in the Birch Gulch region, is also being investigated, but may have been sparked by lightning."

"Do you know how soon it will be before these wildfires are contained, and is the town of Glacier Creek in any danger?"

"We have four crews working the fires, and we've recalled some of our deployed crews, as well. Right now, Glacier Creek is not in danger, but if that changes, we'll issue evacuation orders to those who might be impacted."

Dylan switched off the television. He didn't want to see any more. He'd grab a shower and a bite to eat, and make sure Hayden made it safely back to the campground, and then he'd head over to the base and suit up.

BUT WHEN DYLAN returned to the hospital less than an hour later, both Hayden and the boys were gone.

"Where are they?" he asked the nurse in charge.

"Not sure," she replied, barely looking up from the paperwork she was completing. "She checked herself out about an hour ago."

Dylan drove out to the campground and located the site where the Airstream was parked, but there was no sign of the lime-green Jeep, or Hayden. Where could she have gone?

And then he knew.

Thrusting the Range Rover into gear, he accelerated out of the campground, churning dirt and gravel under the tires. Ten minutes later, he pulled into an empty parking space next to Hayden's Jeep. Neither she nor the boys were in sight. Climbing out of his vehicle, Dylan blew out a hard breath and looked at the building directly in front of where he had parked.

Glacier Creek Police Department.

He saw the boys as soon as he walked in, sitting in two wooden chairs by the dispatcher's desk, and looking uncharacteristically subdued. Ollie's face brightened when he saw Dylan, and he jumped from his chair to launch himself at him, hugging him hard around the waist.

"Hey, guys," he said, ruffling Ollie's hair. He walked over to sit next to Jackson. "Where's your aunt?"

Jackson indicated a hallway on the opposite side of the waiting area. "She went down there with one of the officers."

"Do you know why?"

Jackson nodded. "She's telling them about the fire."

Dylan frowned. "Why didn't she bring you in with her?"

"Dunno. She just said to wait for her."

Dylan approached the dispatcher's desk. Glacier Creek was a small town, and the police force consisted of Chief Clay Willard, eight police officers, an animal control unit, and Raelynn, the dispatcher. She'd worked at the Glacier Creek Police Department for as long as Dylan could remember. A statuesque woman in her mid-forties, she'd been married three times and rumor had it she was looking for husband number four.

"Hey, Raelynn," he said, giving her his most winning smile.

"Hey, yourself, Dylan." She beamed, leaning back in her chair and sweeping him with an appreciative look. "What brings you in here?"

"Well, you of course."

Raelynn gave him a coquettish smile, her ruby lips parting to reveal a flawless set of pearly teeth. "Just because I'm beautiful doesn't mean I'm brainless. I eat boys like you for breakfast, sweetie. Why are you really here?"

Dylan jerked his head in the direction of Chief Willard's office. "Who is Hayden Temple talking to? Chief Willard?"

Raelynn frowned. "The woman with the kids? No, she's talking with Logan Starks. He's the only officer in the building at the moment, and she insisted she needed to speak with someone right away."

Dylan nodded, hoping his relief didn't show on his face. Chief Willard was a bully who took pleasure in treating offenders—even those who hadn't yet been found guilty—with a heavy hand. Various complaints had been filed against the chief over the years, including witness intimidation and tampering with evidence, but the charges never seemed to stick. Personally, Dylan disliked the man, but he also knew better than to get on the wrong side of him. In Glacier Creek, Clay Willard was the law.

Logan Starks was fairly new to Glacier Creek, having relocated to Montana from the Chicago police force. Dylan didn't know the other man very well, but he seemed like a decent enough guy. He hoped he wasn't wrong.

"I need to see Ms. Temple and Officer Starks right now," he said, leaning over Raelynn's desk. "This is important,

Raelynn."

Raelynn leaned forward, and lowered her voice to a loud whisper. "Well, you're going to have to wait, Mr. McCafferty. Nobody interrupts a witness statement."

Dylan narrowed his gaze on the woman. "Who said anything about providing a witness statement?"

Raelynn straightened with a satisfied smile. "She did. She came in here claiming she had information about how the Flat River wildfire got started, and wanted to give her statement."

Well, damn. He glanced over at the boys, who watched him with cautiously hopeful expressions.

"Listen, Raelynn, how long do you think she'll be in there, giving her statement?"

Raelynn shrugged. "Hard to say, really." She gave Dylan a conspiratorial wink. "All depends on what she has to say."

Dylan tried to contain his impatience. "Okay, listen, I'm going to bring the boys down to the Gingersnap Bakery and get them something to eat. If Ms. Temple comes out before I return, can you send her down there?"

"What do I look like, a messenger service?"

Dylan raised one eyebrow. "No, ma'am, but you don't look like a babysitter, either. So if you can't give Ms. Temple that message, I'm going to have to leave those boys here. With you. Looks like they're starting to get antsy."

Raelynn's perfectly plucked eyebrows drew together and she gave an unladylike snort. "Fine. I'll send her down to the bakery."

Dylan grinned. "Thanks, Raelynn. C'mon, boys, let's get out of here."

Outside, the boys fell into step beside him. "Where're we going?" Jackson asked.

Dylan glanced down at them. They obviously hadn't been back to the campground yet. Both still wore the clothes they had slept in, and they looked dirty and tired. Why hadn't Hayden allowed them to shower and take a nap before rushing over to the police station? Hadn't she told him she wanted to wait until the boys had rested? Sure, he'd told her she needed to tell the truth about how the wildfire had started, but he'd agreed it could wait until they'd all had some much-needed sleep. He pushed down his rising irritation.

"Would either of you be interested in trying the best whoopie pies in Montana?"

"Yes!" They both exclaimed the word at the same time.

They made their way down Main Street, toward the water. On the far side of the lake, the skies were still clear and blue, but a thick, orange-brown haze hung over the town. They reached the Gingersnap Bakery and Dylan pushed the door open, setting the tiny bells overhead jangling.

The warm, inviting aromas of cinnamon, sugar, and vanilla enveloped them as Dylan closed the door, and he saw the boys breathe deeply. With its exposed brick walls, wide pine flooring, and dark, vintage furnishings, the bakery had always appealed to Dylan. The fact that the owner, Dana Marshall, baked like a dream didn't hurt, either. Two women sat at a table by the large front windows, enjoying cappuccinos and large slices of chocolate cake, while an older man stood by the cash register, waiting for Dana to ring up his purchases. The boys' eyes widened when they saw the selection of pastries and cakes behind the glass display case.

"Hey, Dylan." Dana smiled, after her customer had left. She peeked over the display case at the boys. "Who are these handsome little guys?"

"Hi Dana, this is Jackson and Oliver. We're hanging out for a bit while their aunt, uh, runs some errands."

"She's at the police station," Ollie said matter-of-factly, never taking his eyes off the confections behind the glass. Jackson gave him a shove.

Dana's eyes widened as she gave Dylan a knowing look. "I see. Well, what looks good?"

Dylan had known Dana for a couple of years. She was engaged to one of his firefighting buddies, and had taken over the bakery after Dot, the original owner, had retired. Originally from Arizona, Dana had come to Glacier Creek on vacation, had met Scott Ross, and had stayed.

"I'll have an iced coffee with cream, no sugar," Dylan said. Bending to peer into the display case, he added, "And give me a big slice of your carrot cake."

The boys each selected a homemade whoopie pie and a tall glass of chocolate milk, and Dylan directed them to a table by the windows while he paid.

"I figured you'd be out there fighting the wildfire," Dana said in a low voice, as she neatly slid an oversized slice of cake onto a pretty plate.

"Yeah, well, I was hiking the Eagle's Bluff Trail when the blaze broke out," he explained. "These boys were with their aunt, and we were all trapped above the fire line."

Dana's expression was one of shock. "I had no idea! I haven't even had a chance to turn on the news. Is everyone okay?"

"Yes, we hiked out this morning, and aside from being tired and hungry, we're all fine."

"Jeez, Dylan," she said, staring at him. "I haven't seen anyone from the base since the fire broke out, so nobody told me. Scott is out there now, trying to contain it."

Dylan nodded. "I'm heading over to the base as soon as their aunt returns. I figure they can use all the help they can get."

Dana placed the three plates and the drinks onto a tray, and slid it toward Dylan. "Did you hear about Cole Tanner's lumber mill? Burned to the ground overnight." She shook her head. "Such a waste. I hope they'll be able to rebuild. They depend on that mill for their livelihood."

Dylan frowned and pushed his wallet back into his pocket. "I'm just glad they didn't lose their homes."

Dana shook her head in disbelief. "It's all so unbelievable. I heard rumors the wildfire was started deliberately. If that's true, there's a special place in hell for that person. So much damage! Those forests will take a long time to recover from this."

Dylan took the tray without responding. It wasn't his place to say anything. Besides, what could he say? Cole Tanner and his family were well liked in town, and people wouldn't enjoy seeing them suffer as the result of someone else's negligence. If Dana knew the wildfire had been started by the same boys who now sat devouring her pastries, he was sure she wouldn't take such a hard stand. But Dylan was afraid the rest of Glacier Creek might not be so forgiving.

Chapter Nine

HAYDEN SAT ALONE in Officer Starks's office and dialed her sister's phone number, gratified when Molly answered on the second ring.

"Molly, it's me."

"Hey, is everything okay?"

Hayden closed her eyes. Surely news of the wildfire hadn't reached New Jersey? "Why do you ask?"

"Well, you only ever call on Thursday evenings. How are the boys?"

"They're fine," she assured her sister. "Listen, I only have a few minutes to talk, and I wanted to let you know we're in Glacier Creek, Montana. But there was an…incident, and in case you see something on the news, I didn't want you to worry."

There was a pause. "What kind of incident? I haven't turned the television on in days."

How to explain? Hayden knew no matter what she said, or how she said it, Molly would see this as Hayden's fault. And she would be right.

"I took the boys for a day hike yesterday, and we got

trapped in the mountains overnight by a wildfire, but we're fine."

"Oh my God!" Molly gasped. "Where are you now?"

Hayden hesitated. "We're at the police station in Glacier Creek. But I need to tell you—"

"The police station?" Molly screeched, interrupting her. "Hayden, what happened? I trusted you!"

"Jeez, Molly, it's not like I planned it," Hayden protested. "Like I said, we're all fine. We were lucky enough to run into a guy who works for the U.S. Forest Service as a wildfire fighter. There were a bunch of us, and he kept us safe, and we hiked out of the mountains this morning."

She left out the part where she had practically passed out in Dylan's arms, and had spent the morning in the hospital.

"I knew letting them go with you was a bad idea," Molly wailed. "Thank God they're safe." There was a pause. "Why are you at the police station? How did the wildfire start?"

Hayden heard the suspicion in her sister's voice, and felt her hackles rise. Molly always leaped to the worst possible conclusion. While Hayden desperately wanted to tell Molly neither she nor the boys had anything to do with the wildfire, that would be a lie.

"Molly, please don't freak out, okay?" Hayden clutched the handheld receiver so tightly her knuckles were white. "The wildfire was an accident. Nobody meant for it to happen."

There was silence. And then Molly erupted.

"Jesus, Hayden, you started the wildfire? Oh my God! I knew this would happen! I knew it! You were a pyro then, and you're a pyro now!"

"The barn fire was an accident," Hayden said tightly, struggling to contain what was left of her composure. Even so, she felt a betraying tightness at the back of her throat, and her eyes burned. "Why do you keep blaming me?"

"You know why!" Molly screamed into the earpiece. "Wasn't it enough Dad died in that fire? Do you have to try and kill my sons, as well?"

"Molly!" Hayden exclaimed, truly shocked.

While she knew Molly blamed her for their father's death, she had never actually said so.

Until now.

But to even suggest Hayden might want to harm either of the boys, when Molly knew how much Hayden loved them, was unthinkable.

"Where in hell is Glacier Creek?" Molly demanded. "I'm getting on the first plane, and I am flying out there to get my children."

"Molly, if you'll just hear me out—"

"I've heard enough."

Molly's voice had turned chillingly cold, and Hayden knew further discussion was pointless. Impossible, really. Not that it mattered. Even if she'd had the chance to tell Molly that the boys had started the fire, Molly would still blame Hayden. She should never have had the matches in her backpack in the first place. She'd already told Officer Starks her story, and it would likely be all over the news before the end of the day. She'd hoped she could tell Molly the truth, and have Molly support her. Hayden thought she could endure anything if someone—anyone—was in her corner. She shouldn't be surprised that Molly was so ready to abandon her, just as she'd done when Hayden was fourteen.

"I'll be in Glacier Creek tomorrow to get my boys," Molly said, and the line went dead.

Hayden replaced the receiver, and covered her face with hands that weren't quite steady. She felt ill as all the old memories came rushing back.

What had happened twelve years ago had been an accident, and a day didn't pass when she didn't think about it. Nobody regretted the incident more than Hayden. After all, she had to live with the tragic consequences for the rest of her life.

But despite what had happened, Molly had never denied Hayden the opportunity to spend time with her nephews, or voiced any reservations about letting them go on this trip. That Molly actually believed Hayden would ever put Jackson and Ollie in danger was incredibly hurtful.

The door to the office opened, and Officer Starks entered, carrying a sheaf of papers. Hayden hastily swiped at her damp cheeks, and sat up straighter.

"Okay, ma'am," he said, as he pulled out his chair and sat down on the opposite side of the desk. Under different circumstances, Hayden might have been bowled over by his dark good looks and muscular frame, but not today. His eyes were sympathetic as he considered her for a moment. "I've filed your statement, and a copy will go over to the lead fire investigator."

"What happens now?" she asked. She hated how wobbly her voice sounded. "Will the boys be taken into custody?"

"That depends on the outcome of the investigation," he replied quietly. "Unfortunately, the rules are different in every case. If the investigation concludes the wildfire is the result of willful negligence or arson, then charges will likely be forthcoming."

"And if they conclude it was an accident? They're just little boys!"

Officer Starks sighed. "There's no clear answer. There's a chance that either you or the boys' parents could face charges, or even be held liable for the cost of the fire containment efforts."

Hayden blanched. She had a small insurance policy, but not much in personal savings. She would lose her job. She would lose her house. She knew Molly and Steve had no extra money. They would blame her. In short, her life would be destroyed.

Again.

Hayden forced herself to remain calm, when her insides felt as if someone had just flipped the switch on a blender. She wasn't sure she could go through this nightmare again, but she didn't have a choice. Not when her nephews were involved.

"Okay, I think that should do it," Officer Starks said. "We'll need to talk with the boys, as well, but their parents need to be present."

"Their mother is coming to get them tomorrow," Hayden said. "Is that soon enough?"

"I don't see any problem with holding off until then," Officer Starks said and set the file down. "Anything you might have forgotten to add?"

Behind her the door opened, but Hayden didn't turn around. "No," she said quietly. "I just want to emphasize that I take full responsibility for what happened. I should never have had the matches in my backpack, and I should have kept a better eye on the boys. I'm the one to blame, not them."

"Hayden—"

At the sound of the deep, masculine voice, Hayden whirled around in her chair to see Dylan standing there. His face registered both compassion and concern. Hayden noted he'd showered and changed into a clean shirt and shorts, and he looked so good she nearly flung herself into his arms.

"What happened to the tin box with the matches, Ms. Temple?" the police officer asked.

Hayden turned back toward Officer Starks. "I don't know. The boys said they dropped everything when they heard Dylan mention the bear, so it's probably still beside the trail."

Officer Starks blew out a hard breath. "Okay, we're done here." He stood up and reached across the desk to shake Dylan's hand. "Hey, Dylan, good to see you."

"Yeah, you too. So what happens now?"

"The fire investigation team is going to want to speak with the boys," Officer Starks said, "but we've agreed to wait until their mother arrives, tomorrow. After that, it depends on what the team finds on site, and what the boys have to say."

Dylan shifted his golden gaze to Hayden, but the look of sympathy she saw there was too much.

She pushed hastily to her feet. "Am I free to go? I really need to get back to the boys."

"You're free to go," Officer Starks confirmed. "But you'll need to remain in town. Understood?"

Hayden nodded. "Of course. I'll be at the Glacier Creek campground, site number eighteen."

Without looking at Dylan, she made her way out of the office and down the corridor to the lobby, where Jackson and Oliver sat waiting.

"Hey, guys," she said, infusing her voice with false cheer. "I'm sorry you've had to wait so long, but I'm done now. How about we get an ice cream, and head back to the campground?"

"Dylan already took us to the bakery," Ollie said.

"We had whoopie pies and chocolate milk," Jackson

added, and handed her a brown paper bag. "We brought this for you."

Peeking inside, Hayden saw a small white pastry box. "That was very thoughtful of you." She slid a cautious glance at Dylan. "Since you've already eaten, I guess we can go straight back to the trailer."

Acutely aware of Dylan following her, she herded the boys ahead of her as she pushed through the glass doors of the police station. They encountered two uniformed officers coming in from the parking lot. The first was an enormous man with a huge gut and a ruddy face beneath his hat. His small eyes narrowed on Hayden as she passed him, and he stopped, nearly blocking her path.

"What have we here? Can I help you, miss?"

Hayden turned, and the leering, speculative expression on the officer's face was hard to ignore. Fine rivulets of sweat trickled down his face. He lifted his hat and swiped his sleeve over his bald head.

"No, thank you," Hayden said politely. Instinct told her she'd been lucky that Officer Starks had been the one to take her statement, and not this man. She didn't like the gleam in his eyes. "We were just leaving."

She felt Dylan's hand at the small of her back, urging her forward. "Chief Willard," he said, with a nod to the other man.

Hayden pushed through the second set of glass doors. As they stepped outside, she heard the chief's raised voice.

"Would someone kindly tell me what in the Sam Hill is going on? Who was that woman?"

"C'mon," Dylan said, his voice grim. "Get your Jeep started and let's get out of here."

But Hayden was already digging her keys out of her backpack. "C'mon, boys," she said, "into the Jeep. Hurry, now."

"I'll follow you back to the campground," Dylan said. His gaze flicked to the boys as they clambered into the back seat. He lowered his voice and leaned down to speak directly into her ear. "You and I need to talk."

Hayden watched as he strode toward his Range Rover, before climbing into the Jeep and turning the engine over. As she drove through Glacier Creek toward the campground, she couldn't prevent her gaze from straying into the rearview mirror at the black vehicle following her.

When they pulled into the campground, she sent the boys into the trailer to take a shower and change into some clean clothes. They dragged their feet, clearly wanting to wait for Dylan to arrive. But as his Range Rover pulled into the small site, she shooed them quickly inside. As Dylan climbed out of his vehicle and strode across the campsite toward her, she swiped her damp palms against the seat of her shorts, suddenly nervous. He caught her by one arm and drew her slightly away.

"Are you okay? The hospital staff said you checked yourself out."

"I'm fine," she assured him, flushing beneath his intense stare. "I was just light-headed this morning, but I feel better now."

"Why didn't you wait for me to return?" he asked, frowning. "I thought you were going to wait to make any statement until after the boys had showered and rested?"

"I just wanted to get it over with," she explained. "I knew I'd never be able to relax or sleep with that hanging over my head."

"I would have brought you to the firefighting base, not the police station." He paused, and gave her a quizzical look. "Why do you feel you're to blame for the wildfire?"

"Because it is my fault," she said, glancing toward the trailer. She kept her voice low. "I completely forgot that I had those matches inside the first aid tin. I should have known better, especially considering—"

She broke abruptly off.

"Considering what?" Dylan asked. "What were you going to say?"

Hayden sat down at the nearby picnic table, her knees suddenly weak. "Nothing."

Dylan crouched in front of her and took her hands in his. "Hayden, I understand you want to protect the boys, but this isn't your fault. They shouldn't have taken the matches from your backpack. They're both old enough to understand what they did has consequences."

The compassion and understanding in his hazel eyes

nearly undid her. She dragged in a shaky breath. "There are things you don't know, Dylan. Things I can't tell you, because if you knew—"

He gave her a crooked smile. "What? I'd think differently about you? Trust me, I have good instincts where people are concerned."

Hayden dropped her gaze to look at her clasped hands. "I just wish there was some way to keep their names out of the news. My sister is on her way to Glacier Creek," she said in a low voice. "She's bringing the boys back to New Jersey tomorrow."

"They're going to be questioned first." He arched one eyebrow. "You know that, right?"

Hayden raised her gaze to his. "Yes, I know. Officer Starks said it can wait until tomorrow. I thought it might be easier for them if their mom was there. I told them they should tell the truth about what happened, but I can't help feeling that if I'd just paid closer attention, none of this would have happened."

His expression was equal parts exasperation and understanding. "Hayden, you can't protect everyone all the time. But for what it's worth, I'll be right there with you."

She nodded, too overwhelmed to form words. But she also knew that while she had his support now, once he learned the truth about her past, she'd lose that as surely as she'd lose him.

Chapter Ten

DYLAN LEFT THE campground feeling frustrated. There was something Hayden wasn't telling him, and he hated that she didn't trust him enough to share whatever was bugging her. He also understood her need to protect her nephews, but she didn't seem to understand the consequences to herself.

Then there was the part of him that admired her, because he knew if he were in the same situation, he might have done the same thing. She'd looked so small and fierce as she'd insisted on taking the blame upon herself that he couldn't help but be a little impressed, even as he'd wanted to shake her.

Or kiss her senseless.

That brought back memories of the morning, when she'd woken up in his arms. He'd stayed awake all night, keeping an eye on the group and ensuring their safety in case the wildfire threatened their location. Hayden had shivered in her sleep, so he had shifted her to a more comfortable position against his chest in an attempt to share his body heat. Afterward, he didn't know what had prompted him to kiss her. He'd wanted to the instant she'd woken up, and the sleepy confusion in her blue eyes as she'd looked up at him had tugged at him, drawing his head down. He hadn't been able to resist kissing her, and even now he couldn't bring himself to regret it.

He pulled into the Glacier Creek base station, noting the dozens of cars already parked there. Sam had called in all available resources to battle the wildfire, and Dylan intended to volunteer, as well. He strode through the entrance doors, and his eyes were immediately drawn to the parachute hanging from the railing of the second-story loft, above him. The red, white, and blue chute was a tribute to the previous base captain, Russ Edwards, who had been killed while jumping a wildfire more than a year ago.

Pushing the unpleasant memories aside, Dylan nodded at Jacqui, who was on the phone, and turned past the reception desk and down the hallway to Sam's office. Sam stood studying a map of the region with two firefighters but looked up as Dylan paused in the doorway.

"Hey, Dylan," he said, straightening. He looked at the other men. "Give me a minute."

He stepped into the hallway, drawing Dylan with him. "What are you doing here?"

"I came to suit up. Tell me where I need to be, and I'll join that crew."

"No," Sam said, shaking his head. "We have enough crews out there. You need to get some sleep, and then maybe

I'll consider using you."

"I know this fire, Captain," Dylan said urgently. "I was right there!"

"And you did a great job getting those hikers out," Sam said, putting a hand on Dylan's shoulder, "but I can't endanger your life or the lives of the crew by putting you on the line in your condition. Go get some sleep. Come back in twelve hours and we'll talk about putting you out there."

Dylan frowned. "Captain, I've gone for days without sleep when we're fighting a fire. One sleepless night isn't going to make a difference."

"Twelve hours, McCafferty."

"Six hours," he countered.

Sam shook his head, but a rueful grin touched his mouth. "Eight hours, and I don't want to see you a minute sooner. Got it?"

"I'm bunking down here," Dylan said, referring to the bunkroom on the upper level of the station.

"Suit yourself," Sam said.

Dylan made his way to the ready room, just down the hallway from Sam's office, and checked his equipment. Nearly all of the individual ready stations were empty, since every available firefighter had been called up, or deployed to another location. Satisfied his gear was in order, he turned to leave the room and nearly collided with Cole Tanner, who was just entering. He almost didn't recognize his friend, dressed in his firefighting suit and helmet, and covered in soot and dirt. Only his blue eyes were recognizable.

"Hey, Cole," he said to the other man. Cole had been a smoke jumper with the base for years, until he'd made a decision to take over his family's timber frame business, instead. He'd stayed on as a volunteer, and it was only then Dylan remembered the Holliday lumber mill had burned to the ground. "Listen, I heard about the mill, and I'm sorry. Is there anything I can do for you?"

Cole pulled his helmet off and rubbed a hand over his sweat-darkened hair. "Thanks. Nah, there's nothing anyone can do. The lumber mill is a complete loss. I'm just glad nobody was hurt, and we were able to prevent the fire from spreading to Eldon's house."

Eldon Holliday was the man who had raised Cole, and Dylan knew his friend looked upon the older man as a father. Dylan found he couldn't look at Cole, knowing how the blaze had started. "Will you rebuild?"

"We had insurance, so we'll rebuild, but most of the timber was destroyed in the fire. Fortunately, Eldon and I recently signed a contract to purchase a tract of forest about twenty miles south of here, so we'll be able to harvest some lumber there."

Dylan nodded. "That's good to hear. How's Joy doing?"

A ghost of a smile touched Cole's mouth at the mention of his fiancée. "Better now that the immediate fire danger has passed, and I'm safe and heading home."

Joy's first husband had died fighting a wildfire in California. It was no wonder she worried every time Cole volunteered at the base.

"Tell her I said hello," Dylan said, "and let me know if there's anything I can do to help you rebuild."

He left Cole and made his way to the bunkroom, where several other firefighters were catching some sleep. Dylan sat down on an empty cot and yanked his boots off, and then set the alarm on his phone to go off in five hours. He lay back on the narrow mattress and closed his eyes, but all he could see was Hayden's face, clouded with anxiety.

He drifted into a troubled sleep but came awake with a start about four hours later. Momentarily disoriented, he realized he was in the bunkroom, and that four hours had passed since he'd set his alarm. From somewhere outside he heard a screech that sounded suspiciously like audio feedback.

Tugging his boots on, he shoved his phone into his back pocket. He was alone in the darkened bunkroom, but he could hear voices coming from downstairs. Walking over to the window, he pushed aside the shade and peered at the parking lot, astonished to see a half dozen television crews assembled there. A makeshift platform had been assembled in front of the fire station, and Sam Gaskill stood there with Chief Willard and several other town officials.

"Christ," he muttered, and sprinted down the stairs, and outside.

Skirting the platform, he made his way to the edge of the

crowd. Dylan recognized a number of townspeople, including his best friend and partner, Jamie Colter. He pushed his way through the crowd, until he stood beside Jamie. He had a clear view of Captain Gaskill and Police Chief Willard.

"What's going on?" he asked Jamie.

"Hey, man," Jamie said, clapping him on the back. "Glad to see you made it back safely. You just missed the Captain extolling your heroism in bringing those hikers down safely this morning."

"Is that what this is about?" he asked, keeping his voice low.

Jamie bent his head to Dylan's. "They're giving a status on the wildfire and the containment efforts, but I heard a rumor they found some evidence."

"Like what?" Dylan thought of the first aid tin.

Jamie shook his head. "I don't know."

Whatever it was, it couldn't be good. He listened in growing unease as Sam confirmed what Jamie had said and told the assembled group of reporters and townspeople that a key piece of evidence had been discovered at the spot where the fire had ignited. A low murmur of excitement ran through the crowd, and several reporters stepped forward, demanding more information.

Dylan frowned as Chief Willard leaned forward to speak into the mike. Even from a distance, Dylan could see the predatory gleam in his small eyes.

"We're working carefully to investigate the circumstances

surrounding the start of the Flat River wildfire," he said. "At this time we do have an incriminating piece of evidence and we also have a person of interest, but we are not releasing any names or additional information until the conclusion of the investigation."

There was a sudden hum of anticipation, and the crowd surged forward as the reporters began to call out questions, yelling in order to be heard over each other in their eagerness to learn more.

"Is the suspect in custody, Chief?"

"How did the fire start, Chief? Was it deliberate?"

"Is the person a local resident?"

Chief Willard held his hands up, ordering the crowd to silence. He stepped forward, shouldering Sam out of the way as he spoke directly into the microphone, eliciting an ear-piercing squeal of feedback.

"As I said, the investigation is ongoing. The person of interest is a twenty-seven-year old woman from Maryland but I repeat—we are not releasing any names at this time." He paused to hitch his pants up higher over his gut. "I can assure you, if this individual bears any responsibility for starting this fire, I will personally ensure she is tried to the fullest extent of the law."

Dylan muttered an expletive. "What a jackass. The guy doesn't even have his facts straight! Worse, he did everything but give out her name and social security number."

Jamie turned to look at him, and his expression turned to

one of astonishment. "Jeez, McCafferty, you know this woman?"

"She was part of the group I brought out of the mountains," Dylan said. "But Willard has it all wrong—she did not start that wildfire. I can't believe he just publicly indicted her! How does that fat bastard keep getting elected?"

Jamie gave a snort of disgust. "He has everyone in the county in his pocket, one way or another. He's a vindictive son-of-a-bitch, no question."

"I'm heading over to the campground," Dylan said. "I don't trust him not to haul her into jail before the investigation is even complete."

Jamie grabbed his arm, halting him. "Wait. *She's at the campground?*" He gave Dylan a look of disbelief. "This isn't the woman with the Airstream, is it? The hot one who almost hit your car?"

"Does it matter?"

"Hell, yeah, it matters!" Jamie pulled Dylan out of the crowd. "I know you like her, but if she played any part in this wildfire, you need to stay away before you get in too deep."

"Don't believe a word Willard says. She did *not* start that fire. I just want to make sure she's okay," Dylan said, his tone defensive. "Right now, I'm her only friend."

Jamie snorted. "Well, you should probably know if her identity gets out—and it will—and you're seen with her, you'll be persona non grata in this town. It won't matter if she's innocent, or not."

"Oh, come on," Dylan scoffed. "I don't believe that."

"You should. Eldon Holliday is a pillar of this community. People love him, and after what he and his family have been through…" He gave Dylan a meaningful look. "I'm just giving you fair warning."

"Understood," Dylan muttered. "Just remember there are always two sides to every story, and you shouldn't believe everything you hear—especially when Chief Willard is doing the talking."

DYLAN WAS HALFWAY to the campground when he passed Hayden's Jeep traveling in the opposite direction. He caught a glimpse of her face behind the wheel, pale and frightened. He yanked hard on his own steering wheel and pulled a hard U-turn, his tires churning gravel on the soft shoulder. Stepping hard on the accelerator, he came up close on her rear bumper and hit his horn, gratified when she put her blinker on and pulled over to the side of the road.

Dylan flung his door open and strode to the driver's side of the Jeep. Hayden looked shaken as she rolled her window down.

"What's going on?" Dylan asked, frowning. "Where are you going?"

"I don't know," she said, and her voice quavered. "We

went to the convenience store to get some groceries, and when we got back to the camper—"

She broke off, and to Dylan's horror, her blue eyes welled with tears. He watched, speechless, as a single tear spilled over her lashes and made a wet trail down her pale cheek. Something twisted in his chest. He could handle almost anything except a woman's tears.

"Hey," he said, frowning. "What's wrong? Did something happen?"

Jackson leaned forward from the back seat, and Dylan saw the boy was both furious and scared. "Someone wrote stuff all over the camper," he said, his voice low with indignation. "With bright red paint!"

"And they smashed out the windows," Ollie added, his eyes round.

Dylan shifted his attention back to Hayden. "Is that true?"

Hayden nodded, and swiped furiously at her damp cheeks. "They took off into the woods when we pulled in, but there were other campers standing nearby, and they started yelling stuff at us—horrible stuff. They just stood by and let those hoodlums vandalize the Airstream!" She stared at him. "Dylan, they *know*."

"They're jumping to conclusions," Dylan said grimly. "Chief Willard identified the suspect as a woman from Maryland, so it's possible someone saw your license plate and decided you're the culprit."

"But I *am* the culprit," she whispered. "Oh, Dylan, what are we going to do? We can't go back there!"

Dylan knew his expression was tight with suppressed anger, and he made an effort to control his emotions. Right now, she needed a friend, and a safe place to stay.

"Have you eaten?" he asked.

"We were about to cook dinner when I realized we needed milk," she said. "We were just coming back when we saw what they'd done to the trailer."

Dylan drew in a deep breath and then blew it out hard. "Okay, follow me. We'll ditch your Jeep at my place, and head into town and grab a bite to eat."

"Maybe I should just check into a hotel," she suggested. "I don't want to involve you."

"The only place around here is the Snapdragon Inn, and they're usually booked three months out. I doubt you'll get a room."

"I could drive down to Bozeman," she said. "That would put me closer to the airport for when my sister gets here tomorrow."

"You're not driving three hours to Bozeman," Dylan said firmly. "C'mon, let's bring your Jeep to my place, and we can figure this out over dinner."

To his relief, she nodded. "Okay. Thanks."

Dylan returned to the Range Rover and climbed inside. He made a quick call to the base station to let them know he wouldn't be able to suit up, but Jacqui assured him they had enough resources on site. But as he pulled ahead of Hayden on the road, Jamie's words kept reverberating in his head.

You need to stay away before you get in too deep.

But Dylan knew it was already too late for that.

Chapter Eleven

HAYDEN COULDN'T PREVENT herself from gaping at Dylan's house as they pulled into his long driveway. There were no rustic, heavy timber cabins in New Jersey or Maryland, at least not the areas where she and her sister lived. Even to Hayden's untrained eye, the house was an architectural masterpiece of massive timber trusses and expansive windows, perched on the edge of a steep overlook.

She climbed out of the Jeep, in awe.

"Is this where you live?" Ollie asked, clearly impressed. The property was nearly invisible from the steep road, shielded by towering pine trees, but Hayden could see the back of the house had unobstructed views of the valley below, and the town of Glacier Creek itself.

"This is it," Dylan confirmed. "I'd invite you to have dinner here, but I don't have much in the way of food." He shrugged. "I'm a bachelor, so the contents of my fridge consist mostly of beer, beer, and more beer."

"That's okay," Hayden assured him. "You've already done so much for us. You don't have to feed us, too."

"I want to have dinner with you," he said. "C'mon, we'll

go to Red's Diner and get a home-cooked meal."

"What about the Airstream?" Hayden asked. "Shouldn't we report the vandalism to the police?"

"I called Officer Starks on the way over here," he said. "He promised to check into it, but it was probably just a bunch of kids." He didn't add how he'd told Starks to keep Willard in line. The vandalism never would have occurred if Chief Willard hadn't made the inflammatory comments about a woman from Maryland. "I wouldn't be surprised if they're tourists, and not even from the area. There's an RV dealer not too far from town, so we'll bring the camper there in the morning, and see if they can repair the windows."

"Can they clean the paint off?" Jackson asked hopefully.

Hayden gave him a one-armed hug. "I'm sure they can, bud."

She pictured again the hateful slurs spray-painted on the shiny exterior of the camper. Words like *bitch* and *firebug* and *whore*. She couldn't imagine the kind of person who would do such a thing, but then again, the people of Glacier Creek probably couldn't imagine the kind of person who would start a wildfire, either.

They drove back into town, and Dylan found a parking spot outside Red's Diner, on the main road.

"Are you sure this is a good idea?" Hayden asked, looking at the bright, fifties-era interior of the restaurant. Already, the place was filled with customers. "What if someone recognizes us?"

"Most of these people are tourists," Dylan said. "They don't know anyone in town. And if there are any locals in there, I promise you they're good people."

Drawing in a deep breath, Hayden nodded. "Okay, I trust you."

Inside, Dylan steered them to a booth near the back of the restaurant. As the boys admired the oldies paraphernalia adorning the walls, Hayden began to relax marginally. Dylan was right; except for a few people who nodded to him, or raised a hand in greeting, nobody paid them any attention. The diner was bright and cheerful, and their waitress was a young woman, probably just out of high school, who clearly knew Dylan. From where she sat beside Jackson, Hayden had a clear view of the counter, and the customers who sat on the shiny red stools, enjoying their meals.

"Wow, this place really has an authentic soda-fountain vibe," she said, smiling at Dylan. "I keep expecting to see poodle skirts and saddle shoes!"

"What's a poodle skirt?" Ollie asked, wrinkling his nose.

Dylan laughed. "Way before your time, little man."

As Dylan and the boys looked at the menus, Hayden eyed a television hanging over the counter, near the waitress station. Even from where she sat, she could see the coverage of the wildfire. The volume had been turned off, but Hayden doubted she would have been able to hear anything over the rock and roll music piped in through the overhead speakers. Still, the sight of the firefighters in their protective gear, silhouetted against the intense orange of the flames, was sobering enough that Hayden lost her appetite.

"What looks good?" Dylan asked, studying her from over the top of his menu.

"Mm, maybe just the soup of the day," she replied, dragging her attention back to the menu. She was certain whatever she ate would taste like ashes in her mouth.

She saw Dylan frown, but he didn't comment. When the waitress returned with their drinks, he and the boys each ordered a cheeseburger—their second that day—with fries.

"Are you sure you won't have something more substantial?" the waitress asked, eyeing Hayden doubtfully. "A strong breeze would blow you away."

"Just the soup," Hayden said. She forced herself to smile, and tried her best to relax, but every person who passed their table caused her to jump. She half expected someone to accuse her of starting the wildfire.

"You doing okay?" Dylan asked, after the waitress left.

Hayden nodded and gave him a bright smile, winking at Ollie. "Of course. We should probably talk about where the boys and I will stay tonight." She narrowed her eyes at him. "Are you sure there are no other hotels nearby?"

Dylan shrugged. "Sure, there are. Just not in Glacier Creek. You'd have to head up toward Whitefish, but this is high tourist season for the park, so there's no guarantee you'd find anything."

Ollie and Jackson watched them both, and Hayden

didn't miss the worry in their eyes.

"Can't we stay with you?" Ollie asked, and looked hopefully at Dylan.

"Well," he replied, looking directly at Hayden, "that was going to be my suggestion."

The thought had occurred to her, too, but she would never have had the courage to ask him if they could crash at his house. But now that he'd offered, she found herself reluctant to accept. It seemed, somehow, too familiar. Too intimate, especially considering she'd spent far too much time thinking about him and how much she wanted to kiss him again.

"Oh, I'm not sure…" she demurred.

"Auntie Hayden," Jackson protested, and there was no mistaking the pleading in his voice. "Where else are we going to stay? Besides, he invited us!"

"And he has a cool house," Ollie chimed in.

"Really, it's not a big deal," Dylan said, giving her an encouraging smile. "There're two extra bedrooms, and there's plenty of room. Tomorrow morning, we'll bring the Airstream to the dealer and get it fixed."

Tomorrow morning.

"My sister will be here tomorrow to pick the boys up and bring them back to New Jersey. I'm not sure what time her flight gets in, or how long it will take her to get here, so maybe we should bring the trailer to the dealer later in the day?"

Jackson groaned and dropped his head onto his arm. "I don't want to leave tomorrow."

Suddenly, Ollie began patting her arm with his hand, trying to get her attention. "Auntie Hayden, look! Look, that's you!"

Hayden followed the direction of the little boy's gaze to the television over the counter, and her mouth fell open.

"Oh my God," she breathed. "How—?"

Dylan turned to see what had captured her attention, and she heard his muttered oath. There, on the television, was a picture of herself. The caption beneath the photo read, "Person of Interest in Flat River Wildfire – Hayden Temple."

Jackson leaned forward, his expression tight with anxiety. "Auntie Hayden, why does it say you're a person of interest?" he asked, his voice little more than a hissed whisper.

It seemed to Hayden the entire diner grew silent as they watched the news report, and saw the face of the person allegedly responsible for the wildfire that had destroyed a lumber mill and threatened a town. Instinctively, Hayden put a hand up to shield her face, in the futile hope nobody would recognize her. The waitress chose that moment to reappear with their food.

"Here you are, Dylan," she said sweetly, as she set his plate down. "And here are your cheeseburgers, boys."

She put Hayden's soup down in front of her with enough force that liquid sloshed over the sides and onto the table. Hayden looked up in surprise, and was astonished by the hostility she saw in the other woman's eyes.

"Here's your soup," the waitress said, her tone morphing from sweet to icy. "I hope you choke on it."

"Audrey, that's enough," Dylan said, a warning in his voice.

"You're right, it is enough," Audrey retorted, and pulled a piece of paper out of her apron. She slapped it onto the surface of the table. "Here's your check."

She turned and walked away, but it was too late. People in the diner had overheard her words, and were beginning to realize Hayden was the same woman whose picture flashed on the television screen. A low murmur ran through the diner as heads turned in their direction.

"I'm not hungry," Hayden said quietly, and pushed her bowl of soup aside. A hot wave of mortification washed over her. She felt ill. She wanted to bolt; to get up and run out of the restaurant, and not stop until she'd put Glacier Creek and the accusing stares of these people behind her. But she knew it would be pointless. She'd already learned you couldn't outrun your past.

"Hey, turn up the volume, would you, Sylvia?" called one of the older men who sat at the counter.

Another waitress retrieved a remote control and switched the volume on; at the same time she turned down the overhead music. Dylan had been in the process of pulling some bills out of his wallet, and now he paused, his attention riveted on the news report. Chief Willard stood beside a reporter, looking red-faced and triumphant.

"As I said earlier, we have a person of interest in regard to the Flat River wildfire. As a matter of course, we conducted a thorough background check on the individual, Ms. Hayden Temple." He paused for dramatic effect. "It has come to light that this person is also responsible for a fatal arson fire in Pennsylvania that claimed the life of one man, and caused extensive property damage."

At that point, Hayden stopped hearing anything except the hard swoosh of her own blood in her ears.

"Dylan," she said urgently. "Let's go. I don't want to see this."

He raised one finger to her, and Hayden wanted to slither beneath the table. She averted her eyes from the television, but she could still hear the broadcaster, and the words she knew would incriminate her in the hearts and minds of the Glacier Creek residents.

Willful negligence.

Fatal fire.

"Auntie Hayden?"

The uncertainty in Ollie's voice broke the spell, and Hayden rose to her feet. "C'mon, boys, let's go."

For once, they didn't argue. Dylan tossed some money onto the table and stood up. Their meals were left untouched. Dylan herded them through the now silent diner, and Hayden thought they might actually make it out the doors without incident, when suddenly a woman sitting at a nearby table pushed to her feet and stepped directly into Hayden's path.

She was older than Hayden, and attractive in a soccer-mom sort of way. She'd been having dinner with her two children, a boy and a girl who looked to be just a few years younger than Jackson and Oliver. They were beautiful children, and now they watched their mother with a mixture of anticipation and apprehension. Hayden could picture the woman volunteering on the PTO, and baking food for the school fundraisers. She was no doubt well liked. A pillar of the community.

"You sicken me," she said now in a low voice, as she glared at Hayden. "My husband works for the forest service." She gestured toward the table where her children watched her, wide-eyed. "My kids hike along those very trails where you started that fire. Look at them! I want you to look at their faces, and tell me how you *dare* come into this town and put them in danger through your negligence. How dare you."

"Peggy—" Dylan tried to interrupt the woman's angry tirade, but she turned her flashing dark eyes on him instead.

"And you, Dylan McCafferty! Shame on you for bringing her in here! For shame! For shame!"

"Okay, that's it," Dylan muttered, and ushered Hayden and the boys past her. "Have a good night, Peggy."

"We don't want people like you in our town!" Peggy

called after their retreating backs.

They stepped out onto the sidewalk, but Hayden could still hear the woman's venom-filled voice, following them out of the diner.

Shame on you!

When she would have said something to Dylan, he put his hand beneath her elbow and steered her toward his Range Rover.

"Just keep walking," he said grimly.

Only when they were inside the Range Rover and heading out of the downtown area did he finally look at her.

"I'm sorry about that," he said. "Peggy Ashton is a big personality in this town, but she doesn't have all the facts, and she doesn't speak for everyone."

"I'm glad she's not *my* mother," observed Jackson.

"She was so mad!" Ollie piped up from the back seat. "I thought she was going to start a fight with you, Auntie Hayden!"

"Well, it's over now," Hayden said, and gave Ollie a reassuring smile, when inside she felt like crying.

"We didn't even get to eat," Jackson complained.

"There's a fast-food joint on the outskirts of town," Dylan said. "We'll go through the drive-thru and bring it back to the house to eat."

Back at his house, the boys ate at the big island in Dylan's kitchen, and then Hayden put them to bed in one of the guest rooms. They'd left the campground without grabbing their pajamas or clothing, so the boys each slept in one of Dylan's T-shirts. She knew they were troubled by the days' events, as they didn't even complain about having to share the guest bed.

"Auntie Hayden?" Jackson asked, as she tucked them both in. "Are you in a lot of trouble because of us?"

Hayden studied his thin face, noting the fear and anxiety in his big, blue eyes. "Of course not," she said. "The news reporters were talking about something that had nothing to do with the wildfire, or with you."

Jackson frowned. "But did you really start that fire they talked about?"

Hayden stroked a hand across his brow, pushing his hair out of his eyes. "Unfortunately, I did," she said softly.

"What does *fatal* mean?" Ollie asked. "The television said you started a fatal fire."

"That means someone died in the fire."

"Was it Grandpa?" Jackson asked. "Mom never talks about it."

"Yes," Hayden confirmed sadly. "It was a terrible, terrible accident and nobody regrets it more than me. But it happened a very long time ago, and I don't want you to worry about that, okay? I'll be right downstairs if you need me."

She kissed them both and stood up, turning out the light, and leaving the bedroom door partially open. Downstairs, the kitchen and living areas were both empty, but the

French doors at the back of the house were open. Hayden stepped out onto a wide deck, and found Dylan sitting in a deck chair, drinking a beer. She moved to the railing and leaned against it, looking at the panoramic vista spread out before them. She could see the lights of Glacier Creek twinkling below them and out on the dark expanse of the lake, a few winking dots of brightness where boats navigated the water.

"This is so beautiful."

"Do you want to tell me what happened?" Dylan asked, ignoring her comment. His tone was mild, but contained an underlying chill.

Hayden tensed, and her fingers curled around the railing. "I'd rather not talk about it."

She turned around as Dylan shot to his feet, and he looked so big and so frustrated that Hayden knew a moment of uncertainty.

"You're going to tell me," he all but growled. "Because I can't help you if I don't know what happened."

Chapter Twelve

DYLAN'S WORDS CAUSED something to tighten in Hayden's chest. That he might still want to help her, after everything he'd already done for her and the boys, was nothing short of amazing to her. If he could do this for her, then the least she could do was tell him why she felt so strongly about protecting the boys from any media coverage.

"Okay, you're right. I owe you that." She drew in a deep breath. "I grew up on a working dairy farm in rural Pennsylvania," she began. "The summer I turned fourteen, my sister was already dating Steve, her future husband, even though he was older than her, and my parents really disliked him. She was hardly ever around, so it was just me."

"Why did they dislike him?"

Hayden thought about how Steve had been in those early days, and a wry smile curved her mouth. "He was the cliché bad boy in a small town. He'd dropped out of high school, rode a motorcycle, drank and smoked, and he generally had a badass attitude that didn't sit well with my father." She looked at Dylan. "In short, he had no future."

"So you spent a lot of time alone." It was a statement,

not a question.

"Yes. It was a really hot day in early August. We'd finished dinner and my chores were done, so my mother said I could have some friends over. One of them had stolen a pack of cigarettes from her older brother and wanted to try smoking them."

She paused.

"Go on." Dylan's voice was deep and smooth in the darkness.

Hayden took a deep breath. She hadn't told this story in a very long time, and she found it hadn't gotten any easier with the passing years. Even now, her chest felt tight and achy, and a painful lump formed in her throat.

"We went out behind the hay barn and we each lit one, but they were so disgusting none of us could finish them so we put them out."

"On the ground?" Dylan asked.

Hayden nodded. "After that, we hiked through the woods to my friend's house, but I didn't tell my mother where I was going." She paused. "My dad had driven into town for some tractor parts. When he came back, the barn was fully engulfed in flames. There weren't any animals inside, but neither my dad nor my mom could find me, and—"

She broke off, unable to continue.

"Your dad went into the barn to make sure you weren't there." Dylan's voice was low, and so full of compassion that something broke free in Hayden's chest.

She nodded, as the tears spilled over. "The roof collapsed," she managed to choke, "and he was trapped inside."

Then Dylan was there, pulling her into his arms and holding her tightly, while she sobbed against his chest.

"Oh, Hayden, Hayden," he said softly, while he rubbed her back with one big hand. "I am so sorry."

For a brief moment, Hayden accepted his embrace, allowing herself to lean against him and absorb his heat and strength. Finally, she lifted her head and swiped at her damp cheeks. "The fire investigation concluded the blaze was started by negligent smoking." A small shudder rolled through her. "I've had to live with the consequences of what I did, but there isn't a day that goes by when I don't think of my dad. I'd give anything—*anything*—to take back what happened."

"It was an accident, Hayden. You didn't mean for it to happen."

Pulling free from his embrace, Hayden stepped back and hugged her arms around her middle, feeling weepy and emotionally overwhelmed by the memories of that day.

"It *was* an accident," she finally managed to say, as she thumbed away a tear, "but that wasn't how the media portrayed it, and it definitely wasn't how our small town—or my family—saw it."

"I get it now. I understand why you want to take responsibility for the wildfire," Dylan said. "Because you don't want your nephews to experience what you endured."

"Losing my father was the worst thing that ever happened to me. But afterward…I don't even have words to describe what I went through," Hayden said, searching Dylan's eyes. "I made a mistake, Dylan. A horrible, tragic mistake, and I'll regret it every day for the rest of my life. But once the results of the fire investigation were made public, I was vilified in the papers and on the local news. My mother never really got over losing my dad, and I had to live with knowing I was responsible for her heartbreak. Even my sister—"

She broke off. Her relationship with her sister had changed after that day. While Molly hadn't cut Hayden out of her life completely, she'd shut her off emotionally, and hadn't disguised the fact she blamed Hayden for their father's death.

"Shh," Dylan said, pulling her close again. "I'm sorry for what you went through, but that's not going to happen with Jackson and Ollie. The people of Glacier Creek are good people. They're not going to do a hatchet job on a couple of kids."

Privately, Hayden disagreed. She recalled again how the waitress and the woman named Peggy had verbally assaulted her. She had a hard time believing they would be any easier on two boys. But right now, with Dylan's arms around her, breathing in the clean, masculine scent of soap and pine and unadulterated male, she thought she could face whatever the future held. She drew on his strength, feeling it seep into her own body.

"Thank you for everything you've done," she said, her voice muffled against his shoulder. "You don't know what your support means to me. I never had that, so no matter what happens, I won't let the boys suffer what I had to suffer."

Dylan put his fingers beneath her chin and tilted her face up so she had no option but to look into his eyes. The compassion and understanding she saw reflected there nearly undid her.

"Hayden," he said softly. "I think you're a brave and generous woman. Your nephews are lucky to have you. I'll talk with Sam Gaskill in the morning, and I know he'll be happy to set the record straight about how the wildfire started. Nobody is going to blame you."

"But those women at the diner—"

"Audrey and Peggy are just two people," Dylan interrupted. "They don't represent the entire town. Audrey can be narrow-minded, but that's because she's still young. And Peggy—" Dylan gave a rueful smile. "Well, Peggy's father has run the barbershop in town for the last forty years. He's called the unofficial mayor of Glacier Creek, but sometimes Peggy thinks she's the one who actually runs this town."

"She was so hateful," Hayden whispered, recalling the hostility in the other woman's voice. "She probably has a gazillion friends in Glacier Creek, and they'll all be ready to judge me and hate me, simply because she does."

Dylan rubbed one hand over her back, between her shoulder blades, until she felt some of the tension ease away. "Chief Willard was out of line suggesting you started the fire. He didn't have his facts straight, and he deliberately misled the press. I promise we'll get it straightened out tomorrow. Meanwhile, I don't want you to worry."

"Thank you," Hayden replied. She drew in a deep breath and expelled it forcefully. "Wow. This has been a pretty intense conversation."

"Sorry," he said. "But I hope you can understand why I needed to know."

"Of course."

"Are you okay?"

Hayden nodded, and laughed softly. "I feel like I could use a stiff drink."

"I can definitely help with that," Dylan said, and gestured toward the French doors. "After you."

Hayden settled for a glass of wine, and Dylan retrieved another cold beer from the fridge, before suggesting they sit indoors. Hayden sat at one end of his deep sofa and kicked her shoes off, before tucking her feet up beneath her and taking a grateful drink of her wine.

"This has been one of the longest days of my life," she said. She looked up at him. "I don't know how I would have gotten through without you."

Instead of sitting at the opposite end of the sofa, Dylan

sat directly beside Hayden, close enough that his hard thigh pressed against hers. Taking her wineglass from her, he leaned forward and set his beer on the coffee table.

"Come here," he said, and Hayden went willingly into his arms. "Something tells me you've had a shortage of hugs over the last few years."

A shortage of a lot of things. Like the feeling she had now with his arms securely around her, and his chin resting on her head. She felt safe.

Cherished.

And that was crazy, because he hardly knew her, and what she'd told him about herself and her past could hardly have endeared her to him.

Suddenly, Dylan pulled back and looked down at her, and a frown knitted his forehead. "I mean, I'm assuming you haven't had a lot of hugs, but maybe I'm wrong. Is there someone special in your life?"

"As in, a boyfriend?" She gave a rueful smile and shook her head. "No." She paused, wondering how to continue. "In fact, you might want to think about putting some distance between us, in case people get the wrong idea. I'd hate for you to be ostracized because of me."

"I can handle it," he assured her. "But that's not going to happen."

"You saw how they reacted in the diner."

"That's not what I meant," Dylan said. "I'm not interested in putting any more distance between us. In fact, I'm kinda enjoying where you are, right now. Right here."

A flush of heat swept through her at the expression in his warm, hazel eyes. "Dylan," she whispered, fixing her gaze on his mouth. "I don't think—"

Whatever words she might have uttered were lost as he lowered his head and covered her mouth with his own. But unlike the kiss they'd shared at the waterfall, this one was hot and so sexy Hayden couldn't prevent the small hum of pleasure that escaped her.

Dylan's mouth was warm and firm, and moved over hers with infinite care, as if he was afraid she might push him away. But she'd spent way too much time fantasizing about this, and even though she knew she should put on the brakes, Hayden pressed closer. Dylan shifted, putting one hand at the back of her head, and deepening the kiss, coaxing her lips apart for the intrusion of his tongue. Hayden welcomed the sweet invasion, and threaded her fingers through his hair, reveling in the thick, honeyed strands. She didn't protest when he eased her back against the cushions, following her with the lean, hard length of his body.

He was over her, surrounding her, devouring her, and she wanted more. With a needy moan, she slid her arms around his neck and arched against him. Through the thin material of his T-shirt, his skin was hot and she could feel the bunch of muscles beneath her fingertips. He was so big, and his kisses did things to her that made her feel overheated and shivery all at the same time.

When he dragged his mouth from hers and trailed a line of moist, lingering kisses along her jaw, she gasped softly.

"Good?" he murmured. His voice was a husky rasp in her ear.

She was incapable of uttering a single coherent word. She could only nod mutely and pull his face back to where she could kiss him again. This time, she was the one who plundered his mouth, using her lips and tongue to explore him, taste him, consume him. He gave a deep purr of pleasure, and his hand moved to her hip, before sliding up to cover her breast.

Instinctively, Hayden moved to give him better access, relishing the sensation of his big palm cupping and kneading her sensitive flesh. Sliding her hands over his back, she found the hem of his shirt and pushed her hands beneath the fabric, stroking his heated skin as she kissed him. Tight knots of desire unfurled and bloomed low in her abdomen, and then coalesced into a throbbing ache at her center. Without conscious thought, she pressed her hips upward, seeking relief from the persistent need building between her legs.

Dylan groaned softly and released her breast, allowing just enough room between their bodies to ease his hand between her thighs. He stroked her through her shorts, and Hayden gasped into his mouth. The sensation of his fingers pressing against the seam of her sex nearly undid her, and she shamelessly made room for him, needing more of the exquisite pressure.

"Pull your shirt up," he growled against her mouth. "I want to taste you."

His words caused a wave of hot, liquid lust to course through her body. Just the thought of this man tasting her made her sex tighten and then bloom with need, flooding her center. With shaking hands, she dragged her shirt up and over her head, even as Dylan continued to stroke her intimately. He pulled back just long enough to look at her. His hazel eyes drifted over her, and Hayden had a moment of uncertainty. Did he find her attractive? She'd always wished for large breasts, but they had never expanded beyond a shallow B-cup. Now she wondered if she was enough. Inspired, she tugged her bra down, exposing her breasts to his hungry gaze, knowing the bunched garment would make her appear more enhanced.

"Christ, you're gorgeous," Dylan said.

His voice was husky, but the compliment was so heartfelt Hayden couldn't help arch a little beneath his admiring stare. But when Dylan bent his head down and gently sucked one nipple into his mouth, all ability to think evaporated. His tongue swirled around the tight bud with expert skill, while his hand continued to stroke between her legs, pressing against the most sensitive part of her. She heard a mewling sound of need, and realized with vague astonishment it came from herself. Having sex with Dylan McCafferty had not been part of her plan, but at this moment, nothing seemed more urgent than having him inside her.

She was unprepared when Dylan abruptly broke off the kiss, and pulled away to sit up. Hayden lay there for a moment, too bemused to move until a gust of fresh air from the open doors wafted over her, cooling her overheated senses. Feeling unbalanced, she pushed herself to a sitting position and pulled her bra back up, covering her nakedness. Dylan sat forward with his elbows braced on his knees as he scrubbed his hands over his face.

"What is it?" she asked, touching his arm.

He angled his head to look at her, and she saw the flush of color that rode high on his cheekbones, and the hunger that made his hazel eyes glow.

"You should go upstairs to bed," he said, his voice like rough velvet. "While you still can."

Hayden realized he had no intention of allowing their physical attraction to go any further. For a moment, she just stared at him, unwilling to accept he could turn it off so easily, not when her entire body thrummed with need.

"Dylan," she began, "I want this. Don't you?"

His laugh sounded just a little bitter. "Oh, yeah. But it wouldn't be fair to you."

"How so?"

Reaching out, he laced his fingers with hers. "You're feeling vulnerable and alone right now, I get it. It's natural for you to feel close to me, because let's face it—I'm the only one who's squarely in your corner."

"But…?"

"But it would just be sex, Hayden, nothing more. And that's not what you need right now."

"How would you know what I need?" she asked, trying hard not to feel rejected, and failing miserably. "Maybe that's all I want, too. Maybe that's *exactly* what I want."

Pulling his hand free, Dylan gave a disbelieving laugh. "Oh, no. That's not going to work. I know your type, and all I can tell you is I'm definitely not boyfriend material."

"I'm not looking for a boyfriend," she countered, tipping her chin up. "Besides, I'll be leaving Glacier Creek as soon as this whole thing is over, so there's no chance of us having a relationship anyway."

"Good," he said roughly. "Because a relationship is out of the question. I have too much going on right now with the business, and it wouldn't be fair to you. So do yourself a favor and go to bed."

Hayden snatched her discarded top from where she'd dropped it, and fled upstairs.

Chapter Thirteen

DYLAN WATCHED HER go, and then swore softly. He was an idiot. He should have taken what she'd offered, and damn the consequences. After all, wasn't that what he usually did? If not for an unexpected—and uncharacteristic—pang of conscience, he could have her lying across his big bed as he explored her lithe body. He could easily spend all night screwing her six ways to Sunday, while giving as much pleasure as he took.

Picking up his beer, he took a hefty swallow, and then another, but no amount of alcohol could assuage the lust that had settled in his groin. Even now, he could picture her in the guest bedroom, removing her clothes and pulling on the T-shirt he'd given her to sleep in. He was halfway to his feet before he realized it, and determinedly turned toward the outside deck. No matter how badly he wanted to, he would not climb those stairs to the guest room.

Outside, he rested his forearms on the railing and stared with unseeing eyes at the town below as he drank his beer.

He shouldn't want Hayden Temple.

Everything about her screamed danger, from her wide

blue eyes to her tight, perfect ass. Even her protective instincts toward the boys were a warning.

He told himself he'd done the right thing in sending her upstairs by herself, even as he mentally kicked himself for letting her go. He wasn't accustomed to putting his own wants and needs aside, especially when the woman involved clearly wanted sex as much as he did.

But he knew he wouldn't feel right about sleeping with Hayden. He'd be taking advantage of her during a stressful time in her life, and they'd both have regrets afterward. He'd been truthful when he'd said he wasn't looking for a relationship. He had a business to run and more trips coming up than he could count. He'd be away more than he was home. He didn't need the added complication of a commitment.

When he did think about having a relationship—one that could last a lifetime—he inevitably thought of his best friend, Jamie Colter. Jamie had been crazy about Dylan's older sister, Rachel, for as long as Dylan could remember, since they were little more than scrawny teenagers and Rachel a fully mature woman of twenty. As a teen, Dylan had been disgusted by Jamie's infatuation. But Jamie had always been certain of his feelings for Rachel, and now that they were married and expecting their first child, Dylan had to acknowledge his friend had been right. What Jamie and Rachel had was the real deal.

That's what Dylan wanted, too.

But as much as he liked and wanted Hayden—really

wanted her—he didn't see how they could make it work. Her entire life was on the other side of the country. His life was here, in Montana. He wasn't even sure he was ready for that kind of commitment.

He thought again about the story she'd shared with him about her father. He couldn't imagine living with that kind of guilt and regret. If she really had been slandered to the degree she'd indicated, he could understand her concern for her nephews. He went back into the house and pulled out his laptop. Knowing he wouldn't get any sleep that night, he did a Google search for a barn fire that occurred in rural Pennsylvania twelve years earlier. If he was going to help Hayden, he needed all the facts.

"SHE SHOULD BE here any minute now," Hayden said, scanning the small groups of tourists who strolled along the wide pier that extended from the end of Main Street, out over the lake.

Jackson and Ollie sat on one of the benches built into the railing of the pier, devouring the hotdogs and fries Dylan had bought for them at a small walk-up fast-food shack that stood near the entrance to the pier. Now he leaned back with his elbows braced on the railing, watching Hayden as she paced anxiously in front of them.

They hadn't talked about the combustion that had flared

between them the previous night, or how close they had come to letting the conflagration consume them both. Hayden had come down to breakfast with the boys, acting as if she hadn't almost had sex with him on his sofa.

"You said she's driving up from Bozeman?" he asked, when she briefly stopped pacing.

"Yes. She should be here by now."

She pulled her mobile phone out of her back pocket and looked at it for what must have been the tenth time in as many minutes.

"She would have called you if she was lost," Dylan assured her. "She'll be here."

"I just want this over with," she said in a low voice. She looked at him, and he saw pleading in her blue eyes. "Is there any chance I can persuade you to walk to the end of the pier and pretend you don't know us?"

"Not a chance."

"It might get ugly."

"All the more reason for me to stay."

She didn't argue, and Dylan didn't miss the flash of gratitude in her eyes, just before they widened in recognition. "Oh, there she is now, and—" Her brows drew together in a frown. "Oh, sugar beets."

Dylan straightened. "What is it?"

"She brought Steve with her."

"Her husband?"

"Yes." The single word came out as a groan.

"I thought they were going through a divorce," he said, searching through a nearby group of people for someone who might resemble Hayden.

"They are, which is why I'm concerned." Her face cleared, and she broke into a bright, false smile, even as the boys leaped from the bench and launched themselves at a couple walking toward them.

"Mom and Dad!" Jackson yelled, and flung his arms around the man's waist, while Ollie hugged the woman.

Dylan struggled to hide his surprise. This was Hayden's older sister? While the two women had the same dark hair and blue eyes, that's where any similarities between them ended. Hayden kept her hair short in soft layers that drew your attention to her wide eyes, and emphasized the delicate bone structure of her face. Molly's dark hair hung in disarray around her shoulders, almost obscuring her features. She looked older than Hayden had suggested, and the deep grooves etched on either side of her mouth suggested she wasn't happy. Where Hayden glowed with good health and vitality, her sister seemed stressed and tired.

"Hi Molly," Hayden said, and gave the other woman a swift, awkward embrace. "How was your trip?"

Molly stepped away and gave her younger sister a hard look. "Seriously? You do realize I'm not here by choice, right? That if it wasn't for you and your negligence, this trip wouldn't have been necessary?"

Dylan didn't miss the look of hurt that flashed across

Hayden's face, and he felt his hackles rise. He stepped forward, ready to intervene on her behalf, but Hayden put a hand on his arm, halting whatever words he might have said.

"This is Dylan McCafferty, the man who brought us safely out of the mountains during the wildfire. Dylan, I'd like you to meet my sister, Molly, and her, uh, husband, Steve."

Dylan knew Steve's type. Even on a beautiful summer day like today, he wore a pair of jeans and heavy boots, and a black T-shirt with the sleeves cut off, revealing muscular arms covered in tattoos. He carried a leather jacket over one shoulder, and a chip the size of Montana on the other shoulder. His dark sunglasses concealed his eyes, and a cigarette hung out of the corner of his mouth.

"C'mon, boys," he said now, ignoring both Hayden and Dylan. "Let's get this over with. With any luck, we can catch an evening flight out of Bozeman and be home tonight."

"The police are expecting you to come by the station before you leave so they can talk to the boys. Would you like me to come with you?" Hayden asked, looking at her sister. "I've already provided them with my statement, so I'm sure they won't need more than an hour or so with the boys. You've come all this way, and the town is so pretty. Maybe afterward, I could show you around a bit."

Molly gave her a look of disbelief. "Really? You want to give us the grand tour of the town you nearly burned to the ground?" She made a scoffing sound. "That should be interesting."

Dylan didn't miss how the boys had gone quiet, their eyes round as they looked nervously between their mother and aunt.

"Yeah, I don't think so," Steve said. He took a long drag on his cigarette, and then flicked it away. Maybe he'd meant for it to land in the water, but it fell onto the wooden planks of the pier, beneath the bench where the boys' lunch sat, half-eaten.

Dylan watched it smolder.

"Your cigarette is still burning," he commented.

"Yeah, so?" Steve's tone bordered on belligerent. "What're you—the fucking fire patrol? It'll go out on its own."

Dylan heard Ollie suck in his breath at the swear word, and he pressed closer to his mother. A surge of dislike for the other man swept through Dylan.

"I'd appreciate it if you'd pick it up and dispose of it properly," he said. "I think negligent smoking has caused enough tragedy, don't you?"

He was unprepared when Steve snatched his sunglasses off and pinioned Dylan with a look of disbelief and aggression.

"What did you just say?" he asked, his voice dangerously quiet. "Because I'm not sure I like what you're insinuating."

Dylan narrowed his gaze on the other man. "It's not insinuation, pal. It's fact. Put out the damned cigarette."

"I'll get it," Ollie said, and before anyone could stop him, he scrambled beneath the bench and tossed the smoking butt into the water. "All done!"

Dylan wanted to wipe the smug smirk from Steve's face with his fist. He shoved his hands into the pockets of his shorts instead, to prevent himself from acting on the impulse.

"I guess you'd better get going," he said coldly. "Officer Starks is expecting you, and then it's a long drive back to Bozeman."

His gaze flicked to Molly, and for just an instant he was taken aback by the expression on her face as she watched her husband. He knew hostility when he saw it, but this went beyond that. This was pure loathing. Then it was gone, and he wondered if he'd imagined it.

"C'mon, boys," she said. "Say good-bye to your aunt and let's go."

"Maybe I should go with you to the police station," Hayden suggested. "I was there, after all, and maybe I could help."

"I think you've done enough already," Molly said coldly. "Boys, say good-bye."

The boys each hugged Hayden, and then Jackson shook Dylan's hand.

"Thanks for everything," he said, and Dylan thought he suddenly looked much older than his eleven years.

"You're welcome."

Ollie was less formal, and flung his arms around Dylan's waist. "I don't want to go. Can we come back and visit?" he asked, his voice muffled against Dylan's shirt.

Dylan crouched down in front of the boy and forced himself to smile. "You're always welcome here, you know that. You and Jackson take care of yourselves, okay?"

Ollie nodded, and then cupped his hands around his mouth and leaned forward to whisper into Dylan's ear. "Please don't let Auntie Hayden get in trouble because of us."

Dylan nodded, his gaze shifting beyond Ollie to where Hayden stood a little apart, her arms hugged around her waist. He ruffled Ollie's hair and stood up. He would have liked for Jackson and Ollie to stay, but he'd be glad to see the last of Molly and Steve.

"Molly," Hayden began, and extended a hand toward her sister.

"I'll call you when we're back in New Jersey," Molly said, and stepped back. "Good-bye, Hayden."

She waited with barely concealed impatience as the boys hugged Hayden, before she took each of them by the hand and turned away. Steve never acknowledged Hayden, and with one last look at Dylan, put his sunglasses on before he deliberately shook a cigarette out of a pack he retrieved from his front pocket. He tore a match from a matchbook and lit the cigarette, and then flicked the flaming match onto the pier, where it went out. He took a deep drag of the cigarette and then deliberately blew out a long breath of smoke.

"Later," he said, and turned to follow Molly and the boys.

"What a fucking dick," Dylan muttered.

Hayden groaned and pressed her fingers against her eyes. "I dislike him so much," she admitted softly. "He's always been like that, so condescending and—and—"

"Dick-like?"

A wry smile curved Hayden's mouth. "Exactly." She sighed deeply. "He's another reason why I can't entirely blame the boys for what happened. They learned fire negligence from the best. I just hope Steve doesn't punish them."

Dylan frowned. "Are you saying he'd hit them?"

"I don't know if he'd go that far, but he'll make their lives miserable."

"The way he's done to Molly?"

Hayden looked at him, stricken. "She did look unhappy, didn't she?"

"More than that," Dylan mused. "She looked like she despises him. Why would she bring him with her if they're going through a divorce?"

Hayden shook her head. "I don't know, unless they're trying to patch things up?"

Dylan couldn't prevent a snort of disgust. "She's better off without him. And what was up with the cigarettes? If I didn't know better, he did it deliberately, just to antagonize me."

Hayden shrugged. "He's always been a rude smoker, and he really doesn't care if other people like it, or not. Once, he lit up in a restaurant and even after the manager came over and asked him to extinguish it, he refused. We were all but thrown out."

Dylan was quiet, considering what she'd said. Part of him wanted to follow them to make sure they actually went to the police station, and didn't just skip town.

Hayden walked over to the bench and gathered up the remnants of the boys' lunch, wadding up the paper and napkins, and tossing them into a nearby trash barrel.

"So what happens now?" she asked.

Dylan glanced down the length of the pier, to Main Street. The shops were open, and people were shopping and having lunch. Except for the dull haze that hung over the town, it seemed a day like any other, but Dylan knew differently.

"No formal charges have been pressed against you or the boys," he said. "Why don't we bring the Airstream in for repair, and then we'll stop by the fire station and get an update, okay?"

"I'm not supposed to leave Glacier Creek," Hayden said.

"Officer Starks said you were to stay in the area, and not leave Montana until after the investigation. I don't think there'd be any objection to you getting your camper fixed, since you're coming back to town afterward."

Hayden drew in a deep breath. "You're right. Okay, let's

go get the Airstream repaired. Maybe a miracle will happen and the investigators will determine the wildfire started from natural causes. At least then I can hit the road and leave Glacier Creek." She gave a humorless laugh. "I know this town will be glad to see the last of me."

But as they walked the length of the pier, Dylan realized he wasn't ready to say good-bye to Hayden Temple. He wanted her to stay in Glacier Creek.

Chapter Fourteen

"I SHOULD AT least try to book a room at the Snapdragon Inn," Hayden asked. "Maybe with the wildfire, they've had a cancellation."

"You think that's a good idea?" Dylan asked. "The news crews were swarming over the campground, just waiting for you to return. Do you think they'd leave you alone at the inn?"

She and Dylan were driving back to Glacier Creek after leaving the damaged Airstream trailer at an RV dealership outside of town. Dylan had gone by himself to hitch up the camper and pull it out of the campground, and had confirmed the reporters and news crews had been lying in wait, and had descended on him like a flock of hungry vultures.

He'd been brooding and quiet when he picked her up at his house, and they'd driven together to the dealership. The salesperson had scarcely been able to hide his curiosity when he'd realized just who Hayden was, but one look at Dylan's face, and he'd kept his questions to himself. He'd promised to have the trailer repaired and the graffiti removed as soon as possible, warning it could take a week or more to get the new windows in.

Hayden had hoped the camper could be repaired sooner. There were dozens of campgrounds around the area, and she was confident she could find a secluded spot where she could lay low and avoid the television crews who hounded her. She didn't think she could stay with Dylan, not after what happened the previous night.

She cringed with embarrassment each time she thought about the erotic encounter on his sofa, which was every ten minutes. She couldn't even look at him without recalling the feel of his hands and mouth on her body.

He'd pretty much told her he'd only be using her for sex. She should feel relieved he hadn't treated her so casually; that he'd had enough respect for her to let her go. But there was a part of her that wanted to use him, too. She wanted the mindless pleasure he could provide, no matter how briefly.

And that's what disturbed her the most.

She wasn't the kind of person who engaged in one-night stands. In fact, she wasn't the kind of person who easily let others get close to her. Her last relationship had been with a guy she worked with at the breezy, waterfront pub during the summers, but it had only lasted for a few months. Since then, she hadn't been involved with anyone, on any level.

But Dylan McCafferty had awakened something in her that she'd thought was gone. He made her believe in the goodness of people again. More than that, he made her want to open her heart to the possibility of a happy ever after.

She could envision that with him.

She kept replaying the sofa scene over and over again in her head, and wishing it had ended differently.

She slanted a sideways look at Dylan, who sat in the passenger side of the Jeep, watching the landscape go by. Afternoon sunlight slanted in through the glass, turning his hair and beard growth into burnished gold. A pulse beat strongly along the side of his neck, and the T-shirt he wore hugged his muscular torso and emphasized the impressive bulge of his shoulders and biceps.

As if sensing her scrutiny, he turned to look at her, but his expression was inscrutable. "Why don't you just stay at my place?"

"Oh, no, I couldn't," she protested. "I mean, thank you, the offer is very generous, but you've already done enough for me and I don't want to put you out."

"Look," he said, and his voice was gruff, "if it's about last night—"

Hayden couldn't prevent a small huff of laugher. "Yes, it's about last night!"

"I told you why we shouldn't sleep together. I don't want to hurt you, Hayden."

She spared him one swift, telling look. "Oh, please. I'm a big girl, Dylan." She gave herself a mental shake. "Anyway, it doesn't matter."

"So you'll stay at my place."

With difficulty, Hayden kept her attention on the road.

"People will assume we're sleeping together." Her hands tightened around the steering wheel. "Won't that bother you?"

"Would it bother you?" he countered.

"I don't live here," she said. "But you do. These people are your friends. Your neighbors. Your coworkers. How are you going to handle it when they start treating you like a pariah? When they start accusing you of sleeping with the enemy?"

From her peripheral vision, she saw Dylan shrug. "I can handle it."

Hayden was silent for several long moments as she considered his offer. She had nowhere else to go. But to stay with him seemed like a bad decision, especially considering how attractive she found him. He'd been right when he'd said she felt vulnerable and alone, but that wasn't a new experience for her. She'd felt even lonelier after her father had died, when it seemed everyone had blamed her for his death.

She'd felt abandoned.

Sharing the story about her father had felt like an enormous weight lifted from her shoulders. Dylan hadn't judged her. He'd been sympathetic and understanding. He'd been a rock in a world that had been tilting out of control. And that was part of the problem.

She liked too much about him. She liked the way he talked to her, and the way he listened to her. Most of all, she liked the way he defended her. She hadn't thought she would appreciate a man being protective of her, but found she liked that about Dylan. He made her feel valued, something she hadn't felt in a long time. Beyond that, there was the physical attraction between them. Hayden couldn't recall wanting anyone the way she wanted Dylan McCafferty.

"The dealership said it could be a week before they have the Airstream repaired," she finally said, not looking at Dylan. "If you're serious about the offer to stay with you, then I accept."

Was it her imagination, or did he seem to breathe a sigh of relief and relax, just a fraction?

"Good," he said. "Then it's settled. Let's head over to the police station and make sure Molly and the boys stopped by. I also want to ensure Chief Willard has his facts straight about how the fire started, and that he makes a public statement that you are *not* a suspect."

They arrived back in town, and a feeling of unease settled over Hayden when she saw how many media crews lined the main street and milled outside the police station and Red's Diner.

"Aw, damn," Dylan muttered. "Take your next right."

Hayden did as he instructed, but it was too late. Her lime-green Jeep was a hard vehicle to miss, and the news crews had caught sight of it. As she turned onto the side street, they were already gathering their equipment and giving chase.

"What do I do? Where do I go?" She couldn't prevent the frantic note in her voice.

"Take another right, then go straight." He indicated a narrow alley that ran behind the shops. "Take a right here, and then a left. We'll head back to my place."

"Do you think Molly and the boys are still in town?" she asked. She couldn't imagine why so many reporters were waiting outside the police station, unless they knew the boys were inside, being questioned about the wildfire.

"I'm sure they're halfway to Bozeman by now. The news crews were probably hoping to get a statement from Chief Willard, and then they spotted you."

Hayden looked anxiously into the rearview mirror, thankful when she didn't see any of the television vans following them.

"I think we lost them."

Dylan snorted. "Sweetheart, this town's not big enough to lose anyone. If they want to find you, they will. The most we did was get a running start. With any luck, we can reach the turnoff to my house before they catch up with us."

"And then what?" Hayden spared him a swift glance.

"We'll stash the Jeep in the garage where it can't be seen, and you'll lay low until this thing blows over."

Hayden knew he was deliberately making the situation out to be less serious than it actually was. He didn't want her to worry, and his generosity and compassion made her feel suddenly weary. She was so tired of pretending; of acting like none of this bothered her.

"Thank you," she said again, glancing at him. "You've been so generous, and I don't know how I'm ever going to repay you."

He slanted her a speculative look. "We'll think of something."

For just an instant, she pictured his strong body covering hers, his muscular limbs entwined with her own as he drove himself into her. If he wanted her to show appreciation, she was more than willing. Warmth seeped into her face as she realized he still watched her.

"I just hope by letting me stay at your place, I'm not coming between you and the people you care about here in Glacier Creek."

He indicated the turnoff to his house. "That won't happen. My family and friends will support you the way they support me," he assured her. "I'm going to drop you off at the house, but I'll be back as soon as I can."

"Where are you going?"

"Back into town to talk with Chief Willard, and I also need to stop by the office." He studied her expression. "Don't worry. Nobody is going to bother you while I'm gone."

They arrived at his house, and Hayden parked the Jeep in the garage, where it would be out of sight of anyone who might venture far enough up the tree-lined drive to actually see the house.

"Make yourself at home," Dylan said. "Help yourself to whatever you want. I'll be back as soon as I can."

Hayden stood on his front porch until the beat-up Range Rover was out of sight, before turning to go into the house.

"Hey, Boomer," she said, and bent down to scoop up the enormous cat who came through the kitchen to greet her. He was the size of a small dog and heavy in her arms, but he purred in contentment as she carried him through to the living room. She stood by the doors leading to the deck, gazing with unseeing eyes at the expanse of lake and mountains spread out before her, absently stroking the cat. From this vantage point, the town of Glacier Creek looked like something out of a postcard, with the white spires of the two churches, and the long pier that extended out over the water. She could see the crisp sails of several boats on the lake, and overhead the clouds were white and billowy.

The smoke that had hung over the town for the past two days had finally begun to dissipate, and it was hard to believe a wildfire had threatened the sweet little town and destroyed a local business, or that even now various news crews prowled the streets, looking for a glimpse of those they believed responsible.

A knock at the front door startled her, and she hastily set Boomer down on the floor. Had they found her? Her first instinct was to duck down behind the sofa, but then she realized there was no way anyone could see this far into the house. Cautiously, she crept into the kitchen and peeked out the window toward the front porch. A woman stood there, holding a covered casserole dish in her hands.

She didn't look like a news reporter, but since Hayden had no clue who she was, there was no way she was going to open the door. But to her dismay, as she stood watching, the woman bent and retrieved a house key hidden beneath a stone planter next to the door. Before Hayden could decide where to run and hide, the front door opened and then the woman was there, standing in the doorway to the kitchen, staring at her in astonishment.

"I'm sorry," she said, frowning. "I had no idea anyone was here. I didn't see Dylan's Range Rover, so I let myself in."

"I'm a—a friend of Dylan's. I'm only here for a few days," Hayden said, clasping her hands together. "Can I help you?"

"I'm his neighbor, Laurel Cavanaugh." She held up the covered casserole dish. "I know he's been pretty busy these past couple of days, so I made him a—" She stopped abruptly, and behind her thick, black-rimmed glasses, her eyes rounded owlishly. "Oh! You're…her! The woman on the news!"

Hayden briefly closed her eyes, knowing recognition was inevitable. She sighed and nodded. "That's me." She put out her hand. "Hayden Temple."

"Oh!" Laurel stared at her extended hand for a moment, before she hastily set the casserole dish on the nearest surface, and then warmly clasped Hayden's hand. "It's a pleasure to meet you."

Hayden couldn't hide her surprise. "It is?"

Releasing her hand, Laurel used a finger to push her glasses up higher on her nose. Glasses that to Hayden looked suspiciously fake. With her auburn hair pulled back in a messy bun, and her shape concealed beneath an oversized shirt, she looked both awkward and endearing as she gave Hayden a self-conscious smile. "If you're a friend of Dylan's, then that's enough for me."

"Wow," Hayden said on a note of wonder. "Dylan told me his friends would be kind to me, but I didn't really believe it until just now. That's very sweet of you, all things considered."

Laurel smiled. "If there's one thing I've learned, it's that there are always three sides to every story."

Bemused, Hayden tilted her head. "Three?"

"Of course. Your side, their side, and the truth."

Hayden stared at her for a moment. "You're right."

Laurel swung her arms, looking suddenly uncomfortable. "Well, I should probably go. I think you've been through a lot in the past few days, and the last thing you need is to entertain me."

"Actually," Hayden said, on a sudden inspiration. "I'd really like it if you could stay for a bit. There's lemonade or iced tea in the fridge, and we could sit outside on the deck. I mean, if you'd like."

Laurel's eyes widened, and her mouth opened in an "*oh*" of surprise, before she broke into a wide smile that completely transformed her features.

"I would like that," she said. "Thank you."

As Hayden retrieved glasses from the cupboard, she felt her spirits lift for the first time since she'd learned the truth about Jackson's involvement with the wildfire. She liked to think her summers spent as a bartender had given her a sort of intuition where people were concerned, and she thought perhaps Laurel Cavanaugh could use a friend.

Truth be told, so could she.

Chapter Fifteen

DYLAN TOOK THE opportunity away from Hayden to stop by the Glacier Creek base station and talk with Captain Gaskill about the fire investigation. He sat in Sam's office, a mug of coffee cradled in his hands.

"We found a metal tin that contained some first aid items, and several wooden matches. The tin was embossed with an ad from a town in Maryland—the same town where Ms. Temple lives—which corroborates what she told Officer Starks."

"So what happens now?" Dylan asked.

Sam shook his head. "I honestly don't know. The boys are so young, I doubt any charges will be pressed against them personally. But the courts could decide to hold either Ms. Temple or the boys' parents responsible." He blew out a hard breath. "It's not up to me."

"They're not even her kids. How can she be held responsible?"

Sam looked at Dylan with renewed interest. "I heard Hayden Temple is staying at your place. Is there something you want to share with me?"

Dylan frowned and looked away, pinching the bridge of his nose. "I just don't want to see her lose everything because of this. She's a good person, Sam. A really good person."

"And you know this how? After just three days?"

Dylan shifted uncomfortably. "I just do."

"She was responsible for watching those boys. She admitted that the matches were hers, and she was negligent in keeping an eye on the kids. Could it happen to anyone? Sure, but this isn't her first rodeo. She was responsible for an arson fire in Pennsylvania. I don't see how you can defend her."

They were interrupted before Dylan could respond.

"Hey, you two should come out here and check out the news."

Both Dylan and Sam looked around to see Scott Ross leaning through the doorway. His expression was grim.

Exchanging a look with Sam, Dylan rose and followed the other two men into the common area, where the firefighters relaxed during their downtime. In addition to some comfortable leather furniture, there was a pool table, a foosball table, and a wide-screen television. More than a dozen firefighters were in the lounge area, watching a news report.

Dylan stood to one side with Sam, and watched as a female reporter stood next to Chief Willard in front of the Glacier Creek Police Department. Under the bright summer sun, his face looked more flushed than usual, and rivulets of sweat trickled along the sides of his neck and beneath the tight collar of his uniform. But there was no mistaking the gleam of victory in his eyes, as he spoke to the reporter.

"Chief Willard," the reporter began, "you previously reported the person of interest in the Flat River wildfire has a history of starting fires. Can you tell us more about that?"

"I suspected there was more to her story from the moment I laid eyes on her," Chief Willard said, hitching up his trousers.

His sidekick and weekend hunting partner, Officer Fenton Poulain, stood just behind the chief, nodding his head at every word the other man said. Dylan barely suppressed a snort of disgust. In his opinion, Officer Poulain was as corrupt as the chief. Both men had once been involved in tampering with evidence, and Poulain had even paid a hefty fine, but neither had been fired. Unbelievable as it seemed to Dylan, both had kept their positions with the police department.

"As I alluded to during yesterday's press conference, the fire investigation turned up a crucial piece of evidence that we now know provides irrefutable proof of the prime suspect's involvement in the Flat River fire."

"I had no idea he could use so many silver-dollar words in one sentence," Dylan muttered darkly. "He's deliberately twisting facts."

The chief went on to describe the barn fire in rural Pennsylvania, adding the victim in the blaze was Hayden's own father.

Sam turned to Dylan. "Well, so much for your new friend being a good person."

"I know all about that fire," Dylan said in a low voice, "and what the chief *isn't* saying about that accident is more telling than what he is saying."

"You sure it was an accident?" Sam arched an eyebrow. "Wake up, Dylan. This girl has you so infatuated, you're willing to believe anything."

"It's not like that," Dylan ground out through gritted teeth.

On the television, Chief Willard continued tearing Hayden down, disparaging her character and her motives, and promising to get to the bottom of how the wildfire really started.

"He knows damned well Hayden didn't start that fire, but the way he's talking about her, the residents of Glacier Creek will be marching through the streets with pitchforks and torches," Dylan bit out. "It'll be a miracle if she isn't lynched."

"If she's a friend of yours," Scott interjected, "then she's a friend of mine. I trust your judgment in character."

"Thanks, Scott. I appreciate that."

Sam considered both men with something like bemusement, before he shook his head and turned his attention back to the television, where they were now showing footage of the fire from twelve years earlier, as well as pictures of

Hayden's late father. A national news network had picked up the story, and Dylan groaned inwardly. Half the country would know about the Flat River wildfire before the day was over.

LAUREL HAD LEFT an hour earlier, and now Hayden sat in front of the television, watching Chief Willard assassinate her character.

Her life was officially destroyed.

She knew it was inevitable the tragic events of her past would be exposed, but the reporters who covered the story made it sound as if the fire in the hay barn had been deliberate. They had really done their jobs well. There were news clips of the small, rural town where she'd grown up, the dairy farm where her family had lived and, finally, a photo of the smoking ruins that had once been the hay barn. These, she'd been able to handle. But the unexpected photos of her father, identified as the victim of her earlier pyrotechnics, had been too much.

Switching off the television, she buried her face in her hands and let the memories of that day wash over her. She recalled again the fear she'd felt when she realized her friend had brought a pack of cigarettes and a lighter with her, pilfered from her older brother's pickup truck. Hayden hadn't really been interested in smoking, but she had wanted to show she was cool, like her friends.

Her mother had been in the kitchen, putting together pies for the church social the following day, and her father had just left for town to pick up some tractor parts. Molly had been nowhere in sight, and so Hayden and her two friends, Evie and Sarah, had gone out to smoke the cigarettes behind the hay barn. The first puff had choked Hayden so badly she'd ground the offending cigarette beneath her foot and promised never to smoke again. Her friends had each inhaled, and Hayden recalled laughing at their resulting coughing fits. Suddenly, they had heard a rustling noise from inside the hay barn and afraid of getting caught, quickly stamped out the remaining cigarettes before running through the woods to Evie's house.

Hayden hadn't realized she would never see her father alive again. That her mother would need to sell the farm and move into town, where she took a job as a waitress at a small chain restaurant. That her sister would never forgive her for what had happened.

That her life would never again be the same.

She'd lived with the consequences of her actions that day. Some days she would wake up, and for just a few moments she would forget. Then the memories would return and the weight of her loss—her guilt—would sit on her chest, crushing her. Her mother had forgiven her, and through the difficult years following the fire, had been her only ally. But her father's death had taken its toll on her mother, aging her quickly.

Blowing out a hard breath, Hayden wiped her damp cheeks and made her way into Dylan's guest bathroom to splash cold water on her face. Looking at her reflection in the mirror over the sink, she hardly recognized herself. Her short hair was an unruly mess. Her skin looked blotchy and red from crying, and her eyes were puffy and bloodshot.

She turned the shower on as hot as she could stand, and undressed. Standing beneath the steaming spray, she let the pulsing water soothe her ragged nerves. Both the shampoo and body wash she found in the shower smelled like Dylan, and she used it liberally. There was comfort in being surrounded by his scent, and it helped to remind her she wasn't alone.

When the water temperature turned tepid, and Hayden thought she had no more tears left, she turned off the shower, and stepped out. She dried off quickly, and wrapped an oversized towel around herself and scrubbed a second towel over her short hair, before using her fingers to comb it into some semblance of order.

Scooping up her discarded clothing, she opened the door and walked directly into Dylan's hard chest.

"Oh!" she exclaimed, and clutched the front of her towel more securely. "I didn't know you were back."

"I'm sorry," he said, and raked her with an all-encompassing look that missed nothing. "I didn't mean to be away for so long, and then when I came in and didn't see you—" He studied her face, and a frown knitted his forehead. "Are you okay?"

"Of course," she fibbed. She was acutely conscious of how she must look, with her damp hair and skin, wearing nothing but a towel. Dylan was too big, too perceptive. If she continued to stand there, he'd soon uncover all her secrets. "I'm just going to put some clothes on."

"You've been crying."

A statement, not a question.

"I saw the news." She gave him a lopsided smile. "I wasn't expecting them to show pictures of the farm, or of my dad. It just sort of got to me, you know?"

"Hayden—"

She put up a hand to forestall whatever words he might have said next. "No, don't say it. Don't be kind to me, or I'll start to cry again, and it's not pretty."

Dylan didn't return her smile. "Go get dressed. We'll talk when you're ready."

She nodded, and fled to the guest bedroom. Despite the warmth of the day, Hayden pulled on a pair of sweatpants and an oversized, cotton sweatshirt. She needed comfort, even if it was only from her clothes. Feeling better, she walked out to the kitchen, where Dylan was working at the counter. He cast a quick, assessing look in her direction.

"You okay?"

Hayden nodded, opened the fridge, and poured herself a tall glass of lemonade. "What are you doing?"

"I've found that a particularly rough day becomes a little easier when you've had a good meal." He turned and handed her a plate. "I can't take the credit for this casserole, but if Laurel made it, then I promise you it's going to taste just as good as it smells."

"She came over earlier and left it." Hayden sniffed appreciatively. "Mm. I love mac and cheese, and this one looks amazing."

"It's the perfect comfort food," Dylan said.

"You know she has a crush on you, right?" Hayden asked.

"What makes you say that?"

"I'm a woman. I know these things. Did you date her?"

Dylan slanted her an amused look. "No. She's just a friend."

"Does she know that?"

"I've never done anything to encourage her," he said with a frown, and poured himself a glass of iced tea. "I can't help how she feels."

"You're right. And it's none of my business, but she seems like a nice person."

"She is, but she's not my type."

Hayden desperately wanted to ask what his type was, but seeing his frown, she lost her courage.

"Why does she wear those awful glasses? She does nothing to make herself attractive."

"Yeah, I don't know," Dylan said, clearly uninterested in

the subject. "She moved here a couple of years ago, but I don't know where from. She keeps to herself, mostly. She likes her privacy." He gave her a meaningful look, and Hayden took the hint and dropped the subject.

They carried their dishes and drinks into the living room, where Hayden curled up on the far end of the big sofa. She was sure she'd have no appetite, but her first bite of the mac and cheese was so delicious, she continued to eat. Dylan switched on the television and they began watching a romantic comedy. Almost before she realized it, her plate was empty.

"You may want to reconsider your relationship with Laurel Cavanaugh," she said, setting the empty dish on the coffee table. "Anyone who cooks like that is a keeper."

"Hayden—"

She put her hands up in surrender. "Sorry. I'm kidding. I just didn't think I was even hungry, but that was delicious."

Dylan set his own plate next to hers, and picked up his glass of iced tea. "You need to eat, and you need to try and stay positive. It's going to get worse before it gets better. You know that, right?"

Hayden nodded. "It's like Pennsylvania all over again. I'm just grateful nobody was injured, or worse."

"I talked with Cole Tanner, who owns the lumber mill. He said they have insurance and they'll be able to rebuild."

"I'm so glad."

She stared blindly at the romantic antics of the couple on

the television.

"What are you thinking about?" Dylan asked.

"I was just watching the movie, and wondering why my life can't be more like that? I'd be so happy if my life played out like a romantic comedy, and not this ongoing drama." She gave a small laugh and cast an apologetic look at him. "Sorry. If my life isn't turning out exactly as I'd hoped, I only have myself to blame."

"So you're saying you'd like more romance in your life?" he asked, arching an eyebrow at her, even as a smile nestled at the corner of his gorgeous mouth.

Warning bells jangled in Hayden's head. He'd already pushed her away once, and he hadn't given her any reason to think he wouldn't do the same thing again. So much had happened in the week since she'd arrived in Glacier Creek. But the one thing that hadn't changed was the way her heart rate accelerated when she was close to this man.

"I'd settle for raw animal attraction," she said, holding his gaze.

Something hot and primal flared in Dylan's eyes. His body tensed, as if he only held himself in check through sheer force of will.

"Hayden," he warned, and his voice sounded constricted.

"Just one night, Dylan," she said, even as her heartbeat quickened. "I want this. I want you."

"If we do this, there's no going back."

But he was already moving toward her, and Hayden was

aware of a heady sense of elation the instant before his mouth claimed hers, and then she ceased to think at all.

Pleasure coursed through her body at the first touch of his lips against hers, sensual and stunning in its strength. She opened her mouth and pushed her tongue softly against his, as she arched helplessly upward. He didn't touch her, just used the weight of his body to press her back against the cushions until she was supine beneath him. He had one hand on the back of the sofa, and one hand on the sofa arm behind her head, keeping the bulk of his weight from crushing her into the soft leather. Hayden's world sharpened, and then shrank so nothing else existed outside of the sweet, urgent mating of his tongue with hers.

Desire spiraled through her, swirling and gathering like tiny sparks from a flint, until suddenly they coalesced into a single, bright, bursting flame. She curled her hands around the column of his neck and threaded her fingers through his thick, silken hair, feeling the heat of his scalp against her fingertips.

He made a sound of approval low in his throat, and deepened the kiss, licking into her mouth the way she was doing to him. The taste of him was excruciatingly sweet as he sank his tongue deeper. He'd lowered himself onto her now, his hips in perfect, agonizing alignment with her own. She wasn't wearing underwear and through the soft fabric of her sweatpants, she could feel his arousal, rubbing against her.

Dylan lifted his mouth and his eyes glowed in the muted

light as he studied her face, intent, before dropping his gaze to the length of her body. Hayden realized she was shifting restlessly beneath him, her body craving his without conscious thought. His hand went to the hem of her sweatshirt and pushed it up until her breasts were exposed to his hungry gaze. He cupped one breast, caressing it with his thumb until the tip was tight and rosy. When he dipped his head and drew her nipple into his mouth, Hayden couldn't prevent her soft cry. The hot, wet pull of his mouth triggered an answering jolt of pleasure at her center.

Still tormenting her breast, he slid his big hand down her midriff, and beneath the waistband of her sweatpants. When he encountered only smooth, bare skin, he lifted his head in surprise.

"You're not wearing anything under these," he said, and his voice was a rough rasp of velvet across her heightened senses.

"No," she agreed breathlessly. She didn't want him to stop; needed him to continue his downward exploration.

His fingers sifted through the soft curls at the juncture of her thighs, and he lifted himself away from her so she could open herself to him. The sweatpants were roomy, providing him with ample space to part her, explore her.

"Christ, you're so wet," he growled, and lowered his head, capturing her mouth in a kiss so deep and so carnal, Hayden thought she might climax from the sheer eroticism of it. Beneath the soft fabric of the pants, his fingers swirled over her, and then entered her. She groaned into his mouth and pushed against his hand, craving more.

She was unprepared when he dragged his mouth away from hers and reared back, fisting his hands in the waistband of her pants.

"I need to see you," he muttered. "Taste you. Let me."

"Wait," she said when he would have dragged the pants down over her hips. She pushed to a sitting position and slid her hands beneath his shirt, pushing the material upward. Dylan obliged her by reaching behind his head and fisting his hand in the fabric, dragging the shirt over his head and tossing it away.

Hayden's mouth went dry. She'd seen him shirtless before, but not like this. Quickly, she pulled her own sweatshirt off and pressed against him, reveling in the sensation of his hot, silken skin against her bare breasts. Her hands went to the buckle of his belt, and her fingers trembled as she tried to work it free. Dylan brushed her away and unfastened the belt and the snap beneath, but no more.

"Come to bed with me," he said. Twin patches of color rode high on his cheekbones, and his eyes were bright with arousal. "I want to do this right."

Hayden wanted to tell him that the way her body hummed with need, he was doing *everything* right.

"Okay," she said, and pushed herself to her knees so they faced each other on the couch. She looped her arms around his neck and pressed her lips to the jut of one big shoulder, licking along his collarbone to the base of his throat. "Let's go."

She was unprepared when he lifted her into his arms, one hand beneath her bottom and the other around her back, as if she weighed nothing. She hooked her legs around his waist and hung on as he stood up and carried her across the house to his bedroom. The room was dark except for the moonlight slanting in through the two overhead skylights.

Bracing one knee on the mattress of his bed, Dylan laid her across the quilt and followed with the length of his body. Bracketing her face with his hands, he kissed her until she was breathless, stroking the inside of her mouth with his tongue.

Lifting himself from her, he stood up and dragged her sweatpants off in one fluid movement. Despite the warmth of the night, Hayden shivered beneath his hot stare.

"I've imagined this so many times," he said softly, "but you're even more beautiful than I dreamed."

Leaning forward, he put his palms on the upper planes of her chest, and slowly drew them down her body, sliding over the rise of her breasts and ribs, the flatness of her stomach, and the curve of her hips to her buttocks, cupping them and kneading the pliant flesh.

Hayden's breath came swift and shallow as she watched him. His eyes followed the path of his hands, and the expression in them made awareness spread across her skin. But when he slid his palms along the underside of her thighs, and urged her legs apart, she was torn between desire and embarrassment.

"Dylan," she breathed, and her hands went instinctively to cover herself.

"Shh," he said, and pulled her arms away, placing her hands on the quilt. "Keep them there."

She lay there, a mass of trembling nerves and aching anticipation, as he smoothed his palms over her knees and along the insides of her thighs until he reached her center. He used his thumbs to gently part her, and Hayden gave a soft moan as he slid one finger over her throbbing core.

"Good?" he asked.

His voice sounded strained, and when Hayden looked at him, his expression was taut with concentration. She managed to make a strangled sound of assent, and then her whole body contracted as he eased one finger, and then another inside her. She felt the rising crest of an orgasm. She was so close, but she didn't want him to finish her, not yet. Not this way.

Reaching down, she grabbed his wrist. "Wait. I want it to be you."

His eyes gleamed in the silvery light. "It is me."

"Inside me. Now." She reached for the waistband of his shorts, and managed to pull the zipper down. He helped her, shoving the shorts down over his hips and shucking his boxers.

He was heavy and hot in her hand, pulsing against her

palm. She smoothed a fingertip over the tip of him, rewarded when she came away with a drop of syrupy moisture. Her own body responded with a flood of liquid heat, and she urged him over her, widening her legs to accommodate him.

"Please," she said in a voice that sounded husky and deep, so unlike her own. "I want you inside me so badly!"

"Soon, baby," he promised, and reached down to retrieve his shorts from the floor, shaking his wallet out of the pocket and flipping it open with one hand, as he braced himself over her with his free hand. He pulled a condom out of the wallet, and tore it open with his teeth, and then he was rolling the sleeve over himself.

He pulled her more fully onto the mattress and then moved over her, kissing her again, a deep, open-mouthed kiss, pushing his tongue against hers until she moaned into his mouth. Reaching down, he touched her again, circling his fingers over her slickness, before easing a finger inside her. It felt exquisite, but Hayden wanted more. When he withdrew his hand and she felt the broad, bluntness of him pressing against her center, she nearly wept in relief.

Pulling her knees back, she gave a soft groan as he slowly sank deeper, stretching and filling her. He slid a hand beneath her bottom and pushed her up to meet him. He was above her and beneath her and inside her, and Hayden clung desperately to him as the pleasure thickened and her entire body flushed.

He broke the potent kiss and trailed his mouth along the

line of her jaw, pressing his lips against her neck, before gently biting her flesh. She shuddered softly in his arms, rocking her hips up to meet him.

"Don't move," he commanded, his breathing harsh in her ear. "I don't know if I can last, you're so tight."

He shifted slightly, and that was all it took. Hayden was lost as pleasure screamed through her, and she contracted hard around his thick length, her body wracked with wave after wave of blinding release.

With a guttural cry, Dylan thrust into her, his face pressed into her neck, his breath coming in harsh pants as he gripped her buttocks and drove himself deeper, again and again, until he gave one loud, agonized groan and stilled. A shudder shook his big frame.

He rolled onto his side, taking Hayden with him and tucking her against his chest. He neatly removed the condom and disposed of it, and then kissed her again, soft and deep.

"You okay?" he asked.

Hayden nodded, and slid an arm around him, burrowing into his warmth. Her body still thrummed with aftershocks from the explosive orgasm, and a lethargy had settled over her, sinking deep into her limbs.

Reaching down, Dylan shook out a soft blanket folded at the end of the bed, and drew it over them both.

"Get some sleep, sweetheart," he murmured.

Hayden's eyes drifted closed and she fell asleep to the feel of Dylan's arms secure around her.

Chapter Sixteen

HAYDEN AWOKE TO a big, warm male wrapped around her. He nuzzled her neck, his beard growth tickling her as he drew his tongue along the whorl of her ear, making her shiver. She could feel him, hot and hard and heavy, pressed against her backside. An answering warmth filled her limbs, and she reached for his hand, dragging it over her breast.

Dylan cupped the pliant flesh, plucking softly at her nipple until it tightened beneath his fingers. He bit gently on the muscle between her neck and shoulder, and she drew in a soft breath. Opening her eyes, she saw it was early. The light filtering in through the windows was still shadowed and cool, but she felt rested.

Turning her head on the pillow, she looked into Dylan's eyes. They were warm and sleepy, and with his tawny hair and sun-burnished skin, he reminded her of a big, sleek cat. He smiled lazily and pressed a kiss against her mouth, even as his hand drifted down the front of her body and lingered at the apex of her thighs.

Of their own volition, her legs parted. He cupped her in

his hand, and Hayden felt herself grow warm in his palm. He pressed softly, and her breathing quickened. When he drew one finger softly down the seam of her sex, parting her, she closed her eyes, savoring the sensation. He took his time, exploring the soft skin of her stomach, stroking his fingers along the indentations where her thighs met her center, touching but not quite caressing the spot where she needed him most. Finally, after agonizing minutes, he slid one finger through her curls, and over her clit. Hayden sucked her breath in, and shifted to give him better access.

He lifted her leg over his hard thigh, opening her, as his fingers continued to play lazily with her, teasing her.

"Dylan," she breathed.

"Just enjoy."

That was the problem; she enjoyed his touch too much. She wanted more. Finally, he circled one finger over the small, aching nub, and she moaned with pleasure. She was melting, and he dipped inside her for more moisture, swirling the liquid over her sensitized flesh.

Then he was there behind her, hard and thick, easing himself slowly into her entrance, while he continued to play with her. He pushed deeper, withdrawing and then surging unhurriedly upward, filling her, until finally he was seated inside her, with her buttocks flush against his thighs. He began to thrust, and Hayden reached back to grab his head, turning her face to kiss him. He licked at her mouth, found her tongue and sucked on it. All the while, his fingers rubbed and swirled over her clit, until the mounting pressure became too much, and she came in hard, tight spasms around him, every muscle in her channel contracting and squeezing him. He kissed her deeper, but didn't stop touching her, wringing every last shudder from her spent body. Only then did he give one last, powerful thrust, and empty himself with a deep groan of pleasure.

They lay entwined, breathing hard for long minutes before Dylan withdrew, and rose on one elbow above her. He kissed her, and she laughed weakly.

"I don't think I've ever been woken up like that before," she said, and stretched languidly.

"I could get used to it," he said, sliding the condom off and dropping it in a small wastebasket near the bed. Before Hayden could respond, he gave her rump a playful slap. "C'mon, let's jump in the shower and then have breakfast. We have a lot to do."

In the shower, standing beneath his rain showerhead, they soaped each other's bodies, hands sliding over slick skin. Hayden marveled over his contours, his muscles, his heavy layers of bone and sinew. She shampooed his hair and massaged his scalp, letting the long strands slide through her fingers like ropes of silk.

Steam swirled around them as he returned the favor, before cupping her face in his hands and kissing her, eating at her mouth until she found she wanted him again. He was ready for her, but she took her time exploring his length, admiring the size and weight of him, and how he pulsed hotly in her palm, and how his arousal fueled her own.

The water was growing tepid, but neither of them noticed as he lifted her and pinned her against the wall of the shower, bracing her there with his forearms beneath her thighs. She curled her arms around his head, holding him close as he lowered her onto his stiff shaft. She was tender from their previous lovemaking, but she quickly forgot her discomfort beneath the friction of his thrusts. She clasped her thighs around Dylan's hips, and he helped her leverage herself up and down in a rhythm that brought her quickly to orgasm. She cried out and clung to his broad shoulders, riding out the waves, until he suddenly pulled out, letting her feet slide to the floor.

"Touch me," he rasped, and brought her hand to his thick, gleaming shaft.

Still throbbing from her own powerful release, Hayden slid both hands over him. He was so aroused that she only stroked him once before he made a strangled noise and jerked in her hands, ejaculating in long, pearly ropes. It was the most erotic thing Hayden had ever witnessed.

He pulled her back beneath the water and they rinsed off, before he turned the faucets off, and grabbed a thick towel, wrapping her in it.

"I think you're trying to kill me," he said, pressing a kiss against her mouth. "But I'm going to die a happy man."

In the kitchen, dressed in a pair of khaki shorts, a tank

top, and a zip-up hoodie, Hayden sat at the island and sipped a mug of steaming coffee as she watched Dylan move easily around the work area, breaking eggs into a frying pan and laying thick strips of bacon in another pan. He hummed absently as he worked, pausing occasionally to touch her, or give her a secret smile. He broke off a piece of crisp bacon and held it to her mouth. When she took it, he rubbed the pad of his thumb over her lower lip, and then bent to kiss her.

Hayden realized she felt happy, but she also knew it was a fleeting happiness, because what chance did she really have with Dylan? They hadn't talked about what they'd shared—the incredible intimacy of it—and Hayden wasn't about to broach the subject, unwilling to hear him confirm that it was just sex. Because, for her, it had been so much more. She hadn't been intimate with anyone in a long time, and being with Dylan had stirred up longings she hadn't been aware she had. Longings for a home of her own. A family.

Someone to love her.

A place to belong.

Only, Glacier Creek could never be that place, because the entire town despised her. Even if Dylan decided she was the one for him, nobody who cared about him would welcome the news. In fact, they'd likely try to talk him out of it.

As they ate, she listened to Dylan talk, watched the expressions on his face, his fluid movements, and wondered how a guy like him had managed to remain single for this long. He wore a short-sleeved, button-down shirt, untucked over his shorts, in a breezy light blue material that strained over the bulge of his biceps. He looked good enough to eat.

"I thought we could go over to my office this morning," he said, digging into his eggs. "I have piles of paperwork I need to grab. We don't have to stay long; I can bring everything back here."

Hayden nodded. "That sounds good. I'd like to see where you work."

She pictured a travel office with a couple of desks and computers, and walls covered in travel posters, and a shelf with snow globes of cityscapes from around the world. She wanted to see where he spent his time, and what he did that filled him with such enthusiasm when he spoke of his business.

She envied him for knowing what he wanted in life, and having the courage to reach out and take it. If only she could say the same for herself, because she realized what she really wanted was Dylan McCafferty.

DYLAN COULD SEE by the expression on Hayden's face that whatever she had expected, it wasn't the gorgeous, old brick building that housed *Adrenaline Adventures*.

"You own the entire building?" she asked in disbelief. "I

thought you might have just a small room."

"My partners and I purchased the place over a year ago," he said, as they reached the front entrance. "We spent about six months renovating it, and turning it into the home base for the business."

"And is business good?" Hayden asked.

"It's starting to pick up. We've had to bring on more staff, and we've expanded our trips to several different countries."

He was being modest, but he couldn't keep the pride out of his voice when he talked about the venture. What had been born of a mutual love of adventure and travel had morphed into a company that was growing by leaps and bounds.

"C'mon inside," he said. "I'll give you the grand tour."

Originally built as a mercantile store about a hundred years earlier, the building had stood empty for almost six years. Now it housed a sporting goods store, an indoor climbing pinnacle, and an equipment rental center with everything from skis and snowboards to kayaks and bicycles.

But the heart of the business was their adventure travel office, where clients could choose whatever extreme adventure package suited their needs. Most of their walk-in clients opted for the punishing four-day cliff-climbing experience, or the multi-day hiking and white-water rafting trips, since those were local. But that was the smallest part of what they offered.

With the help of his sister, Rachel, who had spent years working as a personal concierge for the rich and famous, they also offered extreme adventures around the globe, to include cave diving in the Caribbean, sea kayaking in Croatia, or hiking the Inca Trail in Peru. *Adrenaline Adventures* had been open for just six months, but business was so brisk they'd been forced to bring in additional staff to help handle the increased volume.

Now he pushed through the oversized double doors of the building and stepped into the cavernous interior of the store, watching Hayden's face as she took it all in. Her eyes rounded when she saw the monolithic pinnacle wall dominating the center of the space and rising up three stories to the vaulted glass ceiling above. Constructed to resemble an actual cliff face, as found throughout Glacier National Park, there were a half dozen climbers making their way toward the top, as staff members belayed their ropes.

"Wow," she breathed, her tone echoing the awe in her expression.

Dylan loved the feel of the space, with its brick walls and iron beams, offset by the enormous, industrial windows overlooking Main Street. Kayaks and bicycles hung suspended overhead, and racks of clothing and shelves of equipment filled the first floor. The second floor was an enormous, wrap-around balcony overlooking the climbing wall and the store below, and this was where his offices were located.

"Do you actually know how to do all this stuff?" she

asked, gesturing toward the climbing wall, and then the kayaks and bikes.

"I grew up doing this stuff," he told her. "C'mon upstairs. I'll introduce you to Jamie, and you can check out the shop while I make a couple phone calls."

He paused when she hung back.

"Are you sure that's a good idea?" she asked.

The uncertainty on her face was so unlike the fierce, tender, incredibly brave woman he'd come to know over the past few days, that for a moment he was too surprised to respond.

"Hayden," he finally said, "Jamie is my best friend. It'll be okay. C'mon."

He held out his hand and, after a moment's hesitation, she took it. In the upstairs office, Jamie was on his laptop, replying to client emails. He looked up when they entered, and Dylan didn't miss the swift flash of surprise on his face. But he composed his features so quickly, Dylan wondered if he had only imagined it.

"Hey, Jamie," he said, and drew Hayden forward. He gave his friend a warning look. "I'd like you to meet Hayden Temple."

Jamie pushed to his feet and extended a hand. His smile was wary. "Hey there, Hayden. I've heard a lot about you, and I'm not talking about the B.S. they've been spouting on the news. Dylan speaks highly of you, and I just want to say any friend of his is a friend of mine."

Hayden smiled uncertainly. "Thank you, I appreciate that. Is your third partner also here?"

"Lucas?" Jamie asked in surprise. "No. Right now, he's what you'd call our *silent* partner."

"Our financier, you mean." Dylan looked up from where he thumbed through a pile of mail. "Lucas is on active duty in the Army, but we're expecting him back in Glacier Creek before Christmas."

Dylan didn't add that Lucas Talbot's stepfather was a billionaire who had recently been killed in a car wreck in New York City. Lucas would be the first one to say he had no claim to his stepfather's money, nor would he want any of it. He'd led a privileged life, and while he'd provided most of the capital behind the company, his true passion was the Army. Dylan hoped when he came home for Christmas, they could finally persuade him to take an active role in *Adrenaline Adventures*.

"What's up for today?" Jamie asked, sitting down and stretching his legs out in front of him.

"I wanted to show Hayden the store, and then I thought we'd head over to the base station and find out what's going on with the wildfire investigation." He was quiet for a moment. "I think we all just want to put this behind us so we can move on."

"Yeah, of course." Jamie rubbed the back of his neck, and then offered an encouraging smile to Hayden. "Hang in there. I'm sure everything will work out."

As they left the office and made their way back downstairs to the store, a familiar voice floated up from the area of the climbing wall, and Dylan groaned in dismay.

"You know what?" he said, tugging Hayden to a halt on the open stairs. "Why don't we head out the back way, instead?"

But it was too late. They'd been spotted.

"Good morning, Dylan."

They looked over the railing to see Peggy, the woman from the diner who had been so rude to Hayden just two nights earlier. She watched them descend with an expression of open dislike on her face.

"Good morning, Peggy," Dylan said smoothly, and even managed to smile at the woman. He'd be damned if he'd be accused of losing his temper in his own business, regardless of how unpleasant the customer might be. "I'm glad you don't find me so shameful that you can't come in and enjoy the climbing wall."

Peggy drew herself up, and there was no mistaking her haughty tone. "Believe me, I wouldn't be here if I had any other choice, but my son was invited to come climbing here with some friends, and I said I would pick them up." She clutched her pocketbook more firmly and tipped her chin up. "Normally, my husband would do that, but he's still performing mop-up duty on the Flat River wildfire."

Her steely gaze shifted accusingly to Hayden.

"Well, I'm glad you came in," Dylan replied, and put an

arm around Hayden's shoulders, sending a clear message. "You're always welcome here."

"Actually, we were just leaving," she said. She turned to a group of boys who were watching an older teenager scale the wall. "C'mon, boys."

Dylan watched them go. "How old do you think her kid is?"

Hayden looked at him. "I don't know. Seven or eight, maybe? He looks a little younger than Ollie."

"Remind me to raise the climbing age to thirteen," he said. "That'll teach her to be so snotty."

As he'd hoped she would, Hayden smiled, but it didn't reach her eyes. "Don't do that," she said. "She's only being nasty because of me, and I'm sorry."

"You don't have to make excuses for her," he said. "C'mon. Let's go talk to Captain Gaskill."

"What if they want to press charges?" she asked.

Dylan didn't miss the tremor in her voice. He pulled her into his arms and then bracketed her face in his hands, searching her eyes. "Listen to me. Whatever happens, you don't have to do this alone. I'll be right there with you. I'm not going to abandon you, or let you face this on your own, okay?"

She gave him a grateful smile. "Thank you."

BUT WHEN THEY arrived at the base station, Sam wasn't there. When Dylan asked the dispatcher about his whereabouts, she cast a wary look at Hayden.

"He's at the police station, meeting with the fire investigation team."

Beside him, Hayden tensed.

The news wasn't good, but not unexpected.

"I probably shouldn't tell you this," the dispatcher added, "but I overheard Sam on the phone." She hesitated, and her attention shifted to Hayden. "Based on the evidence and your statement to the police, they're going to hold you responsible for the cost of the containment efforts."

Hayden nodded briskly, but her face had gone pale and Dylan could see the information unnerved her.

"Okay, thanks," he said, and steered Hayden out of the station.

Only when they were back in his Range Rover and driving did he speak.

"Why don't we head over to the police station and talk to Chief Willard? He knows full well you didn't start that wildfire, and I don't see how you can be held responsible for the actions of two children who aren't even yours. He and Officer Starks talked with the boys, so they know what happened." He made a scoffing sound of disdain. "They should put the cost squarely on the kids' father, if you ask me."

Hayden gave him a rueful smile. "I don't think I'm high

on Chief Willard's list of favorite people, and I have a feeling that Steve and Chief Willard are cut from the same cloth." Reaching out, she laid a hand on his thigh. "I don't want to think about the wildfire right now, or what I may or may not have to pay. I just want to spend as much time with you as I can. Chief Willard can wait another day."

Dylan could feel the warmth of her palm through the thick fabric of his cargo shorts and couldn't help how his body reacted, even knowing how completely inappropriate it was to get turned on under these circumstances. He wanted to take Hayden away and make her forget everything except him.

He could easily spend the next two months hidden away in his house, making love to Hayden Temple. She was the sexiest, most complex woman he'd ever known. He wanted to protect her almost as much as he wanted to kiss her senseless.

"Let's go back to your house," she said softly, as if sensing his mood. "We can at least have tonight, and let tomorrow bring what it will."

But as they drove back to his house, he couldn't shake the feeling that somehow, Hayden believed tonight would be their last night together.

Chapter Seventeen

HAYDEN LAY AWAKE long after Dylan had fallen asleep. She lay facing him in the darkness, watching him.

Memorizing him.

In sleep, his face looked younger, his lips parted, his expression peaceful. He lay on his side with one muscular arm thrown over her waist, and she savored the weight pressing her into the mattress. As he breathed out, she breathed in, inhaling him.

The sheet was pushed down to his hips, and her eyes followed the long, muscled lines of his body, taking in the dark tattoo curling over his shoulder and down the length of his arm.

Their lovemaking tonight had been both urgent and tender. Dylan had brought her to orgasm twice before finding his own release. Afterward, he had held her for a long time, until finally, he'd fallen asleep with her in his arms.

Watching him, she felt a hot tightness in her throat, the sting of tears, and determinedly pushed them back. Staying in Glacier Creek had never been part of her plan. Even without the wildfire, her intent had only been to stay for a few days—a week at most—and then keep moving.

She'd never meant to fall in love.

But then, she'd never met anyone like Dylan McCafferty. Despite his assertion that he had no time for a committed relationship, she knew it was too late.

He loved her, too. At least, she thought he did, even if he wasn't aware of it.

And that was why she couldn't stay.

She'd already damaged his relationship with the people in town. She wouldn't risk damaging his fledgling business, or putting him at odds with his friends and family. People like Peggy could be malicious. She was respected in Glacier Creek, and if she decided to boycott *Adrenaline Adventures*, and persuaded her friends to do the same, she could cause the company harm.

Softly, silently, she slid out from beneath Dylan's arm. He muttered in his sleep and rolled onto his back, but he didn't wake up. Quietly, she moved about the room and gathered up her belongings. She didn't have much, and it didn't take her long to creep out to the kitchen and pull on her clothes. Boomer climbed out of his bed, stretching and yawning, and wound himself happily around her ankles, purring his pleasure in having unexpected company. She picked him up and buried her face in his fur, before setting him back on the floor. Glancing at her watch she saw it was just four a.m. Dawn was just hours away.

But Dylan was an early riser, and she wanted to be gone

before he woke up. She would drive to the Glacier Creek Police Station and talk to Chief Willard. Whatever fate awaited her, it was hers alone. She wouldn't involve Dylan.

She had a moment of anxiety as she opened the garage door, but it slid upward on silent tracks, and she was able to put the Jeep in neutral, and roll it out and down the driveway without having to turn on the engine. Only when she was far enough away from the house did she finally start the ignition, and carefully maneuver the Jeep onto the steep road.

Driving toward the town of Glacier Creek at that hour was both eerie and beautiful. The silvery glow of the moon illuminated the dark houses and empty streets. As she neared the downtown, she found herself driving slower, wanting to take in the beauty of the lake and the reflection of the moon on its pristine surface. On the far side of the lake, the mountain peaks were imposing dark shadows against the night sky.

She idled the Jeep near the town pier and admired the beauty for a moment, when something captured her attention. On a side street paralleling the lake, she could see one house with the first floor lights on. Somebody was awake. Only there was something odd about the lights, as they shifted and glowed in an unnatural pattern. As she peered through her windshield, she realized there was smoke billowing out of one of the windows.

Fire.

Without hesitation, Hayden thrust the Jeep into gear and accelerated the short distance to the house. She flung open the driver's door and sprinted across the lawn to hammer on the front door, shouting at the occupants to wake up. Through the first-floor windows, she could see flames shooting up the walls and traveling across the ceiling.

"Hey! Open up! There's a fire!" she shouted. Standing back, she was preparing to kick the door in, when it suddenly opened. A woman stood there in her pajamas, carrying a young boy in her arms. Her face registered absolute terror.

Peggy.

But Hayden had no time to consider that this was the woman who had been so hateful to her, not when the fire was spreading up the staircase behind her.

"Quick," she shouted, pulling at Peggy's arm. "Get away from the house!"

"My little girl is upstairs!" she cried. "I tried to find her, but she wasn't in her bed!"

Hayden's heart plummeted into her stomach. There was no time. "I'll find her," she said. "You go to the neighbor's house and call 911!"

"No! I can't leave Maddie!" Peggy cried.

"You have to get help!" Hayden shouted. "I'll get your daughter!"

Without waiting to see if Peggy would obey her, Hayden turned and entered the burning house. The heat and noise of the fire was incredible, and she put an arm up to shield her face as she made her way to the staircase. Flames licked along the bottom steps and smoke billowed up the stairwell, choking and thick. Hayden knew she had only minutes to find the child, before they would both be overcome by the smoke.

Racing up the stairs, she called the little girl's name.

"Maddie! If you can hear me, please come out! Maddie!"

At the top of the stairs was a long hallway with doors on either side. Hayden stepped through each, looking into the darkened rooms for any sign of the little girl. It wasn't until she came to the third door that she realized this must be Maddie's bedroom. Glancing behind her, she saw the flames were now traveling up the staircase wall and along the ceiling, and the hallway was thick with smoke.

Retracing her steps, she ducked into the bathroom. She snatched a towel from a rack and threw it into the bathtub, turning on the tap until the towel was soaking wet. Wrapping the wet cloth around her shoulders, she ran back to the little girl's bedroom, and began to methodically check any places where a child could hide.

"Maddie, answer me!" she shouted, looking under the bed and behind a large dollhouse. "Maddie, your mother is waiting outside for you, and we need to go!"

There was no answer, and the only sound was the crackle of flames and the rush of heated air from the hallway behind her. Seeing a closet, she yanked the door open, but it was so black inside she couldn't see anything.

"Maddie, are you in here? It's okay, baby, just come out!"

She almost didn't hear the whimper, but the sound of the little cry made her go to her knees and begin feeling her way along the bottom of the closet. Her hand encountered a small, bare foot.

"Maddie!" she cried in relief. "Thank God! Come here, sweetie!"

She found the child's arm and pulled her forward, out of the closet and into her arms. The little girl clung to her neck, crying. She could have only been four or five years old, and weighed nothing in Hayden's arms.

"Shh," she soothed. "It's okay, you're going to be fine." She pulled the wet towel off and wrapped it over the child, covering her head and as much of her little body as she could, tucking the ends around her bare feet. "Okay, listen to me. I'm going to carry you, and I want you to hold on tight and keep your face pressed against my shoulder, okay? Whatever happens, don't look up. Promise?"

The little girl nodded, and Hayden stood up, her heart pounding hard in her chest. She prayed the staircase was still intact, otherwise she would have to lower the child out a second-floor window.

She stepped out of the bedroom and stopped, suddenly uncertain. Smoke filled the hallway, sooty and thick, and Hayden used a corner of the wet towel to cover her nose and mouth. She looked both ways, disoriented. Flames were spreading along the ceiling, and she ducked down, clutching the child against her chest. She made her way toward the staircase, but came up against a solid wall. She'd gone in the wrong direction!

Turning, she made her way down the hallway in the other direction, groping her way through the smoke. She'd been holding her breath, but when she tried to drag air into her lungs, she found only thick, acrid smoke. She began to cough uncontrollably, and fought back sudden panic as she realized they weren't going to make it. Visibility was zero. Her eyes stung, and tears streamed from them. She couldn't see anything. The heat and smoke were intense.

All she could think was she hadn't told Dylan how she felt about him. She'd left him, believing it was for his own good. She hadn't wanted him to be ostracized by the people he cared about, because of her. The decision to leave him had been agonizing, but she'd known it was the right decision. She was falling in love with him, but now he would never know.

Suddenly, ahead of her, there was a glow of light, and she could see the top of the staircase. A man stood in the center of the light, his hand extended toward her. The light around him was so bright he appeared as no more than a silhouette, yet there was something familiar about him.

Hayden went to him.

When she reached the staircase, the man was no longer there, but Hayden didn't hesitate. She plunged down the stairs, holding the little girl as tightly as she could, barely noticing the flames swirling around her legs.

Then she was outside, and hands were reaching for her, taking the child from her, even as she heard the wail of sirens approaching. Hayden collapsed onto the lawn, her lungs on fire as she coughed uncontrollably, gasping for air.

Someone—a neighbor—threw a wet blanket over her and began patting her down. "Your clothes are actually smoking," he said in astonishment. "What you did was incredibly brave!"

Peggy knelt in front of her, clutching Maddie. "I don't know what to say—how to thank you," she said through her tears. "You saved my little girl."

Then the fire trucks were there, and Hayden watched in a kind of detached stupor as they began pulling equipment from the trucks and battling the house fire. Flames were shooting out of the upstairs windows.

"The man who helped me," she managed to croak, grasping Peggy's arm. "I didn't see him come out. Where is he?"

Peggy gave her a bemused look. "What man, honey? There was no man. My husband is on an overnight shift at the firehouse. He isn't home."

"There was a man," Hayden insisted, her voice barely audible. "He showed me the way out."

"No, I promise you, nobody else went into the house after you," Peggy said.

There was no chance to say more as a coughing spasm overtook her, so strong she doubled over, struggling to breathe. A firefighter crouched in front of her and applied an oxygen mask to her face, and she looked up to see Captain Gaskill watching her with a mixture of admiration and concern.

"That was an incredibly brave thing you did," he said quietly. Then louder, to the emergency personnel who swarmed the property, "Can I get a stretcher over here?"

Hayden tried to protest she didn't need a stretcher, but found she couldn't talk, and she didn't have the strength to argue. As they were lifting her into the back of an ambulance, she heard a man's voice, urgent and commanding, carry over all the other noise.

"Where is she? Hayden! Hayden!"

And then he was there, climbing into the ambulance beside her, his expression both frantic and relieved as he swept his gaze over her, as if he couldn't believe she was alive.

"You crazy, foolish woman," Dylan said gently, putting a hand on her head, and stroking his thumb along her hairline. "What did you do?"

Hayden couldn't help it; her eyes filled with tears that had nothing to do with the smoke. "What I had to."

They both knew they weren't talking about the rescue.

"Ah, sweetheart." Dylan lifted her hand and pressed his lips to her palm. "I've never been so scared in my life. Shh, don't try to talk," he said. "We'll have time for that when this is all over."

Hayden knew she needed to tell him how she felt, before

it was too late. Back in the house, when she'd thought she wouldn't escape, he was all she could think about.

His gaze traveled the length of her body, and Hayden saw him frown. He looked at the paramedic who sat on the other side of her stretcher. "Can you give her something for the pain?"

Hayden wasn't aware of any pain, and tried to say as much to Dylan. She tried to tell him she was okay, and that she loved him, but her voice wouldn't work. She couldn't speak.

Then there was no opportunity. The medic slid a needle into her arm, and a warm rush of heat spread through her body. Her eyes drifted closed, and she knew nothing more.

Chapter Eighteen

HAYDEN WOKE UP, blinking against the sunlight slanting in through the windows to her left. She stared around her for a moment, trying to gain her bearings.

She was in a hospital bed, in a room filled with flowers and balloons, and several stuffed animals. An intravenous drip was attached to her arm, and a slender oxygen tube hooked around her ears and fed oxygen into her nose. Frowning, she pushed herself to a sitting position, wincing at the unexpected pain in her legs.

Dylan sat in a chair next to her bed, his eyes closed. He was too big for the small piece of furniture, and his body was canted at an awkward angle. As she shifted, his hazel eyes opened, and a smile creased his face. He straightened, looking tired and disheveled, but his expression was warm.

"Hey," he said softly, leaning forward. "You're awake."

"How long have I been here?" Her voice came out as a hoarse whisper. She tried to pull the oxygen tube away from her nose, but Dylan stopped her.

"Leave it," he said. "You inhaled a pretty good lungful of smoke, so until the doctor says you're clear, just keep it in place."

Hayden let her hand fall away. "What time is it? Who sent all these flowers?"

"You've been here since they brought you in this morning," he said. He glanced at his watch. "That was about six hours ago. How do you feel?"

Hayden moved experimentally. All the nerve endings in her legs felt as if they were on fire. "What happened?"

"Do you remember the house fire?"

Memories came flooding back. "Yes. The little girl—how is she?"

"She's fine, not a scratch on her, and it's all because of you. You saved her life."

"Thank God," she breathed. "Otherwise her mother would really have a reason to hate me."

Dylan laughed softly. "I think it's safe to say she's had a change of heart. Don't try to talk, sweetheart. The doctor said it'll be a few days before your voice returns fully."

"My legs—" She lifted the blanket and peered underneath. Her legs were wrapped in gauze.

"You suffered first- and second-degree burns," Dylan said. "You were wearing shorts, and the staircase was fully engulfed. Thankfully, the doctors say they should heal with minimal scarring."

Hayden nodded, recalling the events of the previous night, especially before the house fire. "Dylan, about last night—"

He leaned forward and took her hand, lacing his fingers with hers. "Yeah, about last night. I thought what we had was pretty freaking amazing. So what happened? Why did you leave?"

"I didn't want to leave," she said quietly, searching his eyes, letting him see the truth in her words. "But I see how people treat you when we're together. Being with me will only hurt you, Dylan."

To her astonishment, he gave a soft laugh and brought her hand to his mouth, and pressed a kiss against her palm. "Being with you is going to kill me, no doubt about it," he teased. "After the other night, it's a miracle I can even move today."

"Dylan!" She tried to snatch her hand away, blushing, but he held it firmly.

"Sweetheart," he said, "don't you get it? Not being with you would hurt a whole lot more than anything the people of Glacier Creek could dish out."

"Dylan," she said, softer this time. "There's something I've been wanting to tell you—"

"Hey, this is a family hospital," someone said from the open doorway of her room.

They broke guiltily apart, and Hayden looked up to see Captain Gaskill and Jamie Colter standing in the doorway, both of them grinning. Jamie carried a bouquet of flowers, which he sheepishly held up for her inspection.

"I'll just put these over here with the others," he said,

and crossed to the window, where at least a dozen other bouquets and flowering plants made a colorful display.

Captain Gaskill stood at the foot of the bed, his hands jammed into his pockets. "How're you feeling?"

Hayden nodded. "I'm okay."

"Good. What you did was very brave. If you hadn't gone in for that little girl, I doubt we would have reached her in time. You saved her life."

"Do you know how the fire started?" Dylan asked.

"We did a preliminary investigation, and it looks like the microwave oven had a faulty electrical connection. Peggy said she made popcorn before she went to bed, and noticed an electrical odor, but everything seemed fine."

"I'm glad her little girl is okay," Hayden said.

Reaching out, Captain Gaskill picked up the remote control for the television hanging on the opposite wall. "I think you're going to want to see this. They've been replaying it on the news station all morning."

He switched on the television and quickly flipped through the stations until he found a local news channel. Hayden's fingers tightened around Dylan's when she recognized Chief Willard and members of the wildfire investigation team assembled in front of the Glacier Creek Police Station, for yet another press conference.

"Oh, no, please," she said, "turn it off. I don't think I can handle that right now."

"No, you need to see this," Captain Gaskill said.

"Watch," Dylan said, and a smile curved his mouth.

Jamie sat on the edge of the windowsill, his arms crossed over his chest while Captain Gaskill turned up the volume. As the chief talked, a picture of herself came up, and she realized they were calling her a hero for spotting the house fire in the middle of the night, and for risking her own life to save little Maddie.

But when Chief Willard stepped aside and motioned for someone to step up to the podium, Hayden gasped in shock and her hands flew up to cover her mouth. There, on television, stood her sister, Molly, clutching Jackson and Oliver to her side.

"My sister, Hayden Temple, really is a hero," Molly said clearly, looking directly into the camera. "Not only did she save that little girl without any thought for her own safety, but she also sacrificed her own good name for these two little boys, right here."

Jackson gave his mother a tremulous smile, and drew himself up. Molly whispered something in his ear, and then he leaned up to speak into the microphone.

"Everyone thinks my auntie Hayden had something to do with the wildfire, but she didn't." His face flushed red, and his chin trembled visibly, and for a moment it appeared he might cry. Then he squared his shoulders. "I started the wildfire. I took a tin box out of my aunt's backpack, and I was playing with the matches, lighting them and dropping them in the woods while she was looking at a map. I thought

I had put them all out, but I guess not." He looked at his mother, who gave him an encouraging nod. "I'm really sorry, and I'll work every summer to help pay back the money it cost to put out the fire. But please don't blame my aunt, because she didn't do anything wrong."

He looked so young and yet so brave as he stood in front of all those cameras, Hayden thought her heart would burst with love and pride.

"Oh, Jackson," she breathed. "Buddy…you didn't have to do that."

"He's a good kid," Captain Gaskill said. "I spoke with Chief Willard, and no charges will be pressed, based on his age."

She looked at Dylan and saw the truth in his eyes. He gave her a shrug. "I'm not going to say I told you so, but…"

"You did tell me," she acknowledged, smiling through a haze of tears. "I should have listened to you, but after what I went through as a kid, I couldn't take the chance of something similar happening to the boys. I was ready to take full responsibility for the wildfire, if it meant shielding them from the media."

"I get it. But you don't have to worry about that now," Dylan said, smiling into her eyes. "It's over."

"Well, not quite." Captain Gaskill gave her a conspiratorial wink. "I think the town of Glacier Creek may have something planned to show their thanks for what you did."

"Oh, no," Hayden protested. "That's not necessary. Really."

Suddenly, Jamie straightened, his eyes on the door. "Hey, I think you have company."

In the doorway stood her sister, Molly, with Jackson and Ollie. Molly's expression was cautious, as if she was uncertain of the reception she would receive.

"Are you up for more visitors?" she asked. "Because I don't know how much longer I can keep these two away."

"Molly!" Hayden said, and then extended her arms to the boys, who ran into the room and clambered onto the bed to hug her.

"Easy, guys," Dylan cautioned, lifting Ollie away from her legs. "Your aunt has some burns on her legs."

Jackson hugged her tight around the neck, and Hayden could feel his hot tears. "I'm sorry, Auntie Hayden," he whispered.

Hayden squeezed him back. "No, I'm sorry. I should never have had those matches in my backpack. This is on me, not you."

He pulled back and looked at her. "I'm sorry I stole the matches."

"I know you are," she assured him. "But we all learned something from this, didn't we?"

He nodded, and Ollie crawled across the bed to snuggle himself against her shoulder. Hayden barely noticed when Jamie and Captain Gaskill left the room, but when Dylan stood up to go, she grabbed his hand.

"I think maybe you should have some privacy," he said.

"I want you to stay," she said, pleading with her eyes.

"Yes, please stay," Molly said, and Dylan slowly lowered himself back into the chair. Reaching into her pocketbook, she pulled out several dollars. "Boys, why don't you go get yourselves a snack from the vending machine, okay? I need to talk to Auntie Hayden for a minute."

Jackson groaned. "Not again!"

But Ollie scrambled from the bed and eagerly took the money, while Jackson followed more slowly. "How long this time?"

"Give us ten minutes," Molly said.

Hayden sat up a little higher, apprehensive in spite of Molly's recent announcement on television. She could still hear the chill in her sister's voice from their encounter on the town pier.

"Where's Steve?" she asked.

"He flew back to New Jersey yesterday," Molly said. "We never actually went back to the police station after we left you on the dock. Steve flat-out refused."

Hayden stared at her in disbelief. "So where did you go?"

"The boys and I spent the night in Bozeman, and then drove back here this morning, before we even knew about the house fire."

"So what made you come back?"

Molly perched on the side of Hayden's bed. "You never actually told me the boys were responsible for starting the fire. Thank goodness Ollie has never been able to keep a secret. We hadn't even reached Bozeman before the whole story came out. I wanted to turn around right there and then, but Steve refused." Her face twisted in bemusement. "Why didn't you tell me what happened?"

"I didn't see the point. You were so ready to believe the worst of me." Hayden knew her tone was bitter, but she couldn't help herself.

"I would have believed you," Molly said. She bowed her head and picked at an invisible bit of lint on her slacks. "You see, I haven't been entirely truthful with you, either."

Hayden frowned, but when her sister raised her head and she saw the tears welling in her eyes, she knew a moment of panic.

"What is it?" she asked.

Molly swiped at her eyes and made a sound of frustration. "God, this is so hard! I don't even know how to begin!"

"Molly, just tell me!"

"You didn't cause the barn fire that killed Dad! There, I said it!" Molly dragged in a deep, shuddering breath and then blew it out. When she looked at Hayden, her eyes were pleading. "Forgive me, Hayden. I'm so sorry."

Hayden stared at her, unable to comprehend what she'd just heard. "What did you say?"

"You didn't start the fire in the hay barn!" Her voice dropped to little more than a whisper. "Steve did."

Beside her, Dylan made a low growling noise of displeasure.

"*Steve?* But how?" Hayden asked in disbelief. "He wasn't even there!"

"Yes, he was. We both were. Steve and I were in the hayloft—" She broke off, and a flush of color rose in her neck. "We were—you know. Anyway, we heard you and your friends laughing below us, and Steve went down to chase you off."

Hayden dragged up the memories from that day, recalling the noise she and her friends had heard from inside the barn. "That was Steve we heard?"

"Yeah. I was still in the hayloft, but I watched him climb down and walk out to the back of the barn. You and your friends were already gone. Steve lit a cigarette and stood out there smoking for a little while. Then he left, and I went into the house."

"But how do you know it was his cigarette that started the fire?"

Molly was silent for a moment. "The hay loft door was open, and I could see him. He flicked his cigarette away without putting it out first. Like he always does. I didn't really think anything of it at the time."

Hayden stared at her sister, horrified. "Why didn't you say anything?"

Molly began to cry in earnest. "Because I'd just found out I was pregnant! I was only seventeen and I was scared out of my wits! I thought if I told the police he did it, he'd break up with me, and I didn't want him to go to prison! He was twenty-one, and you were only fourteen—I knew they wouldn't press charges against you, and I was right. I'm so sorry!"

Hayden closed her eyes as a tumult of emotions washed over her.

Anger.

Disbelief.

Crushing grief.

Then Dylan's strong arms were around her, pulling her against the solid wall of his chest. She didn't even realize she was crying until his voice penetrated the fog surrounding her brain.

"Shh, don't cry," he murmured, one big hand cradling the back of her head. "I'm right here."

She allowed herself a brief moment to absorb his strength and comfort. Pulling out of his arms, she looked at her sister. She couldn't keep the furious bitterness out of her voice. "Why? *Why?* If you knew Steve did it, why did you treat me so horribly all these years? Why did you push me away? Why did you let me believe I was responsible? All these years…do you know what I've gone through?"

"I do." Molly's voice was so low, Hayden had to lean forward to catch the words.

"And you!" she said, her tone filled with accusation. "You just turned your back on me! You let me take the blame, and never even tried to be there for me. Didn't you know how much I needed you?"

Molly gave a soft sob. "I'm sorry. If I pushed you away, it was because of my own guilt. I've carried this horrible secret around inside of me for so long now, and I'm just so tired of the lies." She wiped her face. "It's just one of the reasons I'm divorcing Steve. He wants me to keep quiet, but I can't. Not anymore." She hesitated. "Can you ever forgive me?"

Conflicting emotions raced through Hayden. She didn't know how she could ever forgive what her sister—and Steve—had done. The fire had robbed her not only of her father, but her family and friends, as well. She'd been emotionally abandoned when she was just fourteen. Her father's death had gutted her, but she'd had to live with the crushing guilt of believing it was her fault. But now Molly was asking for forgiveness—and the chance to repair their relationship.

"All these years," she breathed in disbelief. "I've carried the guilt of his death for almost thirteen years, Molly! I was dragged through the media and shunned by my so-called friends. I was only fourteen, and I went through hell! And now you want me to forgive you?"

"I know," Molly said tearfully. "I won't blame you if you want nothing to do with me."

Nothing could bring her father back, but maybe now she could let go of the guilt she'd carried all these years. In spite of her sister's betrayal, she missed Molly and wanted to be a part of her life. Of the boys' lives. There was no way Hayden could refuse.

"You're my sister," she said simply.

Molly gave a small cry, and then they were hugging each other tightly, both of them crying.

"I have something to tell you, too," Hayden said, when she could finally speak. "Something really...strange happened." She paused, wondering how to tell Molly and Dylan what she had seen, without either of them thinking she'd lost her mind. "I found Maddie, but I became really disoriented in the smoke, and couldn't find my way to the staircase."

"Jesus, Hayden," Dylan muttered. "Disorientation is one of the leading causes of firefighter deaths in structure fires."

Hayden drew in a deep breath, which sent her into a coughing spasm.

"Here," Dylan said, and reached for an inhaler on the nearby table. Holding it to her mouth, he gave it a push. "Just breathe slowly...easy...that's it."

When she could breathe again without coughing, she nodded. "I'm okay, thanks."

"What happened?" Molly asked.

"When I was in that house last night, and I couldn't find the staircase, I was sure little Maddie and I were going to die. I couldn't breathe; I couldn't see anything because the smoke was so thick. And then..."

"What?" Molly asked.

"I saw a man standing in a halo of light. I know it sounds crazy, but at the time I thought it was a spotlight from a rescue vehicle outside. I couldn't see the man's face, but he showed me the way out. He was *beckoning* me. I wouldn't have found the staircase if it wasn't for him."

"Hayden, sweetheart," Dylan said. "You were suffering from oxygen deprivation. It's not uncommon to see things that aren't really there. Both Peggy and Captain Gaskill assured me nobody went into the house after you. The fire department didn't even show up until after you had made it out. There's no way you could have seen anyone standing at the top of those stairs."

Hayden gave him a tremulous smile. "I know. Because it wasn't a man. Not really." She looked at Molly. "I think it was Dad."

Molly's eyes rounded. "*What?*"

"I think—no, I *know* it was Dad, showing me the way out."

Molly covered her mouth with a hand that trembled. "Oh, Hayden."

The boys chose that moment to come back, stepping cautiously into the room and then stopping when they saw Molly's and Hayden's faces.

"Are you *crying*?" Jackson asked, frowning.

"Happy tears," Molly assured him, and put out a hand to him.

"Really?" Ollie asked doubtfully, coming to stand close to Hayden's bed. "You're happy, Auntie Hayden?"

"Yes," she said, and smiled at him. But when she reached

out, it was Dylan's hand she sought. He captured her fingers in his own, and as she looked into his eyes, she realized it was true. She was happier than she could recall being in a very long time.

Chapter Nineteen

"READY?"

Hayden drew in a deep breath, and then blew it out hard. "I'm not sure. The town doesn't need to do anything to thank me."

Dylan glanced out the window of the Range Rover toward the Glacier Creek base station. The grounds of the station had been transformed into a festive carnival, and two enormous party tents had been set up in the parking lot. Dylan could see most of the base crew were manning an assortment of grills and food stations, and people were beginning to arrive and sit down at the dozens of tables and chairs that had been arranged beneath the tents. Families made their way through the carnival's midway, and even from the parking lot, Dylan could hear the shrieks of people on the carnival rides.

A band played beneath the second tent, and a small dance floor had been set up in the center of the tent, surrounded by tables. A group of children were dancing and running around in front of the band, and there must have been a thousand lights strung up around the tents. Beyond the base station, the lake shimmered under a brilliant summer sky.

"Hayden," he said, "you're not giving yourself enough credit. You risked your life to save the life of a child. A child whose grandfather happens to be the mayor of Glacier Creek."

"The *unofficial* mayor," Hayden corrected with a smile.

"Even so," Dylan said, "Maddie's father is one of our own firefighters, and her mother is—well, she was willing to believe the worst of you, and she didn't treat you very well. I think they *need* to do this."

Following the house fire and Molly's televised revelation that it had been her two young sons who had started the Flat River wildfire, the entire town of Glacier Creek had come together to plan an event that would serve as both a fund raiser for Peggy and her family, as well as a way to honor Hayden's selflessness.

A week had passed since the house fire, but Dylan still couldn't completely let go of the fear he'd experienced when he'd learned Hayden had gone into the burning house to save a little girl. His phone had begun to ring in the middle of the night, pulling him out of a deep sleep. Hayden hadn't been in bed beside him, and at first he'd thought she might be in the bathroom. But as he'd listened to the voice on the other end of the phone, his heart had started to hammer with dread.

Jacqui, the base station dispatcher, had taken the initial,

panicked call from Peggy's neighbor, who had said the Ashton house was on fire. When Jacqui had learned Hayden and Peggy's little girl were still inside, she'd called Dylan. At the time, he hadn't been able to make sense of the call. Why would Hayden be on the other side of town at this time of night? And why would she be involved in a house fire? There had to be some mistake.

But as he'd quickly dressed, calling Hayden's name and getting no response, the truth had hit him with all the force of a sledgehammer.

She had left him.

He had no recollection of getting into his Range Rover, or driving to Peggy's house. He only knew as he drove like a madman, he'd prayed to every entity he could think of to keep her safe. When he'd arrived to see the house fully engulfed, the sight had been like a knife slicing through his heart. All he could think was Hayden was somewhere in that conflagration. As a firefighter, he knew her chances of getting out alive—or at least unscathed—were zero to nil, since she had no protective gear, and no firefighting experience.

He'd practically torn the door off the Range Rover in his haste to get to the scene, sprinting across the lawn toward the house. When someone had grabbed him and told him Hayden was safe, he'd nearly gone to his knees in weak relief. But it hadn't been until he'd actually seen her and held her, that his heart had slowed its frantic tattoo.

She was safe.

That was the only thing that mattered. They could figure the rest out later.

That had been just over a week ago. Molly and the boys had flown back to New Jersey the day before. Privately, Dylan thought Hayden had been generous in forgiving her sister so quickly, but that was just one of the things he loved about her. She had a sweet and generous nature. He didn't know if he'd ever fully forgive Molly for what she'd put her sister through, but he'd try for Hayden's sake. When he thought about what she'd endured, his heart ached for her. He couldn't erase what had happened in her past, but he could promise he would be there in her future.

"You won't leave me alone, right?" she asked now, her eyes pleading.

"I told you I'd be there for you, and I meant it. I'm not going to leave you. C'mon, it's going to be fine."

She hesitated, and Dylan leaned across the center console to press his mouth against hers. She sighed and leaned into the kiss, and Dylan smiled against her lips before pulling away.

"Let's do this."

WHATEVER HAYDEN HAD expected, it wasn't the warm welcome she received from the residents of Glacier Creek. As she and Dylan made their way through the crowd, one person approached them, and then another, until Hayden lost count of how many people came forward to introduce themselves, and then thank her for her courage.

There was Laurel Cavanaugh, who gave her a brief hug, and then led her to one of the tables beneath the first party tent.

"I knew there was more to your story than you let on," she said with a knowing smile. "I have a nose for mysteries."

Hayden laughed. "So I understand. I'm sorry I didn't recognize your name; Dylan tells me you write bestselling mystery novels."

"I should thank you," Laurel smiled. "You've provided me with an idea for a new book."

They sat at the table with Dylan's partner, Jamie Colter, who introduced her to his wife, Rachel.

"When are you due?" Hayden asked, indicating the other woman's protruding stomach.

Rachel laughed and put both hands over her impressive baby bump. "Not soon enough! I feel like a beached whale."

Jamie leaned over and kissed her softly. His blue eyes shone with pride. "How many times do I have to tell you, you're the most beautiful woman I've ever seen?"

Hayden watched, amused and touched, as Rachel actually blushed in response to her husband's attention.

"I'm due in four weeks," she finally said, playfully pushing Jamie away, but there was no mistaking the love in her eyes.

"C'mon," Dylan said, putting an arm around Hayden's shoulders. "I want to introduce to some other people." He leaned in and whispered directly into her ear. "And show you off."

The rest of the afternoon passed in a blur. Hayden met so many townspeople over the next several hours, she lost count of how many, and knew she would never remember all their names. There were Beth and Eldon Holliday, who assured her the lumber mill would be back up and running by the end of the year. Then there was Cole Tanner and his fiancée, Joy, and her sweet little daughter, Piper. There was Dana Marshall, owner of the Gingersnap Bakery, and her fiancé, Scott Ross, who Hayden recognized as one of Dylan's friends and fellow firefighters. Then there was Mia Davies, who owned and operated the Snapdragon Inn.

"You know," she said as an aside to Hayden, while Dylan was chatting with Scott and Dana, "the inn is a pretty special place."

"I haven't seen it yet, but Dylan said you're fully booked through the rest of the summer and into the autumn," Hayden replied. "He said the inn is beautiful."

"Oh, it is," Mia said, giving her a conspiratorial smile. "We have quite a lot of weddings there, and it's a popular honeymoon destination."

To Hayden's dismay, she felt her face go warm with confusion and embarrassment. "Oh, well, that's wonderful, but—"

She broke off, unsure how to continue. Dylan hadn't even told her he loved her. Why would Mia think the two of them had any plans for marriage?

"Well, just keep it in mind if you ever need a wedding venue," Mia said, and took a sip of her lemonade, looking at Hayden over the rim of her glass with innocent eyes.

Dylan returned to her side. "They want you to come up on stage."

Hayden looked up to see Captain Gaskill standing on the stage with the band, alongside the entire Ashton family.

"C'mon up, Hayden," he said into the microphone, and the assembled crowd of people began to clap and encourage her to go up.

Dylan caught her hand and carefully led the way, expertly weaving through the tables. Hayden acknowledged the many thanks and pats of encouragement she received, until finally, they stood on the stage next to Captain Gaskill.

Looking out at the assembled sea of people, including many faces she now recognized, Hayden realized this was what she had been missing—a sense of community.

A sense of belonging.

She barely heard anything Captain Gaskill said, until Dylan gently nudged her forward. Only then did she realize the fire captain held a necklace in his hands: a broad red ribbon with a heavy gold medal attached. Now he placed it over her head. Hayden lifted the medal and looked at it. Inside the traditional firefighters' emblem of a Maltese cross were the words *Civilian Medal of Honor for Bravery.*

"Today is your day, Hayden Temple," he said. "The town of Glacier Creek thanks you for your bravery."

The crowd erupted in applause, and Hayden numbly accepted Captain Gaskill's handshake. The Ashton family came forward to thank her, and Hayden bent down to hug little Maddie, who gave her a toothless grin.

"Mommy says you're my guardian angel," the little girl said, when Hayden released her.

"I'm so glad I was there for you," Hayden said.

She accepted Peggy's embrace, amazed at the transformation in the other woman.

"You know," Peggy said, pulling back to smile at Hayden, "the local elementary school has been searching for a full-time art teacher. If you're interested, I could set something up with the school board. We could really use someone like you in our community."

Hayden didn't know how to respond. "That sounds like a wonderful opportunity," she said. "Can I let you know?"

"Absolutely."

As the Ashton family filed off the stage amid much clapping and cheering, Hayden turned to Dylan.

"Oh, Dylan," she said. Overwhelmed by the outpouring of support, she moved into his arms and kissed him in front of the entire town, barely aware of the renewed applause and whistles that went up from the crowd.

"Be careful," Dylan warned softly, smiling against her

mouth. "People might get ideas."

Hayden pulled back to search his eyes, and what she saw there made her breath catch, and gave her hope. She hadn't yet told Dylan what she'd wanted to say the night of the house fire; she was falling in love with him. *Had* fallen in love with him.

Hard, and fast.

But she couldn't trust herself to say the words. Not here. Not yet.

The band had struck up a slow love ballad, and Dylan took her hand and led her back down to the dance floor, where other couples were already swaying together in time to the music.

"Dance with me," he said, drawing her into his arms.

Hayden slid her arms around his neck, and he pulled her close. One big hand was at her waist, and his other slid across her shoulder blades. Heat from his body seeped through the thin layer of his shirt, warming her. As they circled slowly, he bent his head in to her neck and breathed deeply.

"How are you doing?" he asked.

Hayden's lower legs were still swathed in bandages as her burns healed, and she wore a long, flowing maxi dress to conceal them. Her skin was still painful and tight, but less so each day.

"I'm doing great," she assured him.

"I love the way you smell," he murmured into her hair.

"Mm," she agreed. "I love the way you smell, too. Like

pine forests."

Pulling back, he cupped her face in his hands and searched her eyes. "I don't want you to leave Glacier Creek. I'm falling for you so fast, sometimes it scares the shit out of me. But the thought of losing you scares me even more. The night you went into that burning house? I never want to experience anything like that, ever again." A heartbeat passed. "Is there any chance I can persuade you to stay here, with me?"

Hayden stared into his warm, hazel eyes, hardly daring to believe he could be serious. "Dylan—"

"I know we haven't known each other very long," he continued in a rush, as if he expected her to protest. "But we're good together, Hayden. *Really* good."

Hayden searched his eyes. "There's nothing I want more than to stay here with you. I've been trying to figure out how to tell you that I'm falling in love with you, too."

She watched as realization transformed Dylan's face. She didn't know if he was going to laugh or cry. In the end, he simply kissed her, and she was good with that.

"I'll need to bring the Airstream back to the East Coast," she said, when she could speak again.

"No problem," he assured her. "We can make the drive together."

"I have a job and an apartment back in Maryland."

"You could have a job here. I'm crazy about you, Hayden," he said, tipping his forehead to hers. "I want you to stay in Glacier Creek, but it's your decision. If you'd rather stay in Maryland, we can still make it work."

Hayden's head was spinning. Everything was moving so fast, but she didn't need to think twice about being with Dylan.

"I want to stay here," she told him, laughing. "I will stay!"

Dylan grinned and hugged her, lifting her off her feet and kissing her hard, before he set her down. "This is where you belong," he said, and his eyes gleamed warmly.

As she moved back into his arms, and the music swelled around them, Hayden knew he was right.

She was finally home.

The End

The Glacier Creek Series

Book 1: *A Hot Montana Summer*

Book 2: *The Firefighter's Slow Burn*

Book 3: Coming soon

Available now at your favorite online retailer!

About the Author

Karen Foley admits to being an incurable romantic. When she's not working for the Department of Defense, she loves writing sexy stories about alpha heroes and strong heroines. Karen lives in New England with her husband, two daughters, and a houseful of pets.

Thank you for reading

The Firefighter's Slow Burn

If you enjoyed this book, you can find more from all our great authors at TulePublishing.com, or from your favorite online retailer.

Made in the USA
Columbia, SC
09 July 2018